Judas Cross

Judas Cross
Jeffrey M. Wallman

Random House: New York

Copyright © 1974 by Jeffrey M. Wallmann

All rights reserved under International and Pan-American Copyright Conventions. Published in the United States by Random House, Inc., New York, and simultaneously in Canada by Random House of Canada Limited, Toronto.

Library of Congress Cataloging in Publication Data
Wallmann, Jeffrey M
  Judas Cross.
  I. Title.
PZ4.W2148Ju [PS3573.A4395]   813'.5'4   73–20601
ISBN 0–394–48843–1

Manufactured in the United States of America
9 8 7 6 5 4 3 2
First Edition

To W. T. Grant's,
Dale Systems, Inc.,
and the enforcement, penal and judicial authorities
of Passaic County, New Jersey,
without whom this book would never have been written

Behold, I cry out of wrong, but I am not heard:
I cry aloud, but there is no judgment.

                                                Job 19:7

Judas Cross

1-a

Dan Brashear said, "I'm Zig-Zag."

The thin young man at the table yawned. "Yeah, I saw the Corsican on the back of your jacket. So what?"

"So you're Pryce, aren't you?"

"Maybe."

Brashear leaned both hands on the table, almost upsetting the man's bottle of Rheingold. "I'm in no mood to play games, Pryce, not tonight I'm not."

"Neither am I, but you're new to me."

"Mouse passed the word I was coming, didn't she?"

"That don't mean diddly-shit. Where'd you see her last?"

"Tenino Street house."

"She still there if I want to call her?"

"You'll have to call damn loud. There's no phone there."

"Oh yeah. I must've forgotten." The man leaned forward, out of the shadows and into the silver dollar of dim light coming from the overhead spotlamp. He was heavily pockmarked, and was wearing flared cords and a high-collar shirt, a bright red scarf dangling from its open throat like a lolling tongue. Unkempt, greasy hair curled around his collar, while his still greasier eyes slid warily over Brashear.

Brashear was a tall, meaty man looking to be in his late twenties, with thick black hair and a scroungy beard surrounding a hard, hawkish face in a shaggy frame. He had on a black leather jacket which smelled vaguely like dry rot, it not being the shiny kind festooned with doodads, but the older type with the sheep-muff collar and stretch-wrist sleeves and single fly-front zipper. On its back was a scarred, peeling emblem of Zig-Zag cigarette papers, a favorite among roll-your-own pot smokers. His Levi's were filthy enough to stand on their own, and fit snugly over Engineer boots that had church keys hooked into their buckle straps.

As he continued to study Brashear, Pryce thought: He's a hog rider. No Honda or scrambler bike for him; he's probably got some motherin' Harley-Davidson 74 out back somewhere. There'd be a knife on him, too, a German paratrooper's maybe, and his belt would be made of motorcycle sprocket chain, easy to slide out of the loops. Pryce didn't figure on a gun, which was his mistake.

"You finished?" Brashear asked tightly.

"Hang limp, I like making sure."

Brashear straightened, pursed-lipped and feeling rankled. This was a silly thing for the man to be doing, and a sillier thing to say while doing it, and it just went to show you what kind of brains you had to deal with these days. It wouldn't be much of a contest with a punk like Pryce, not as long as he kept him on the defensive, but there'd be the pleasure of taking him out of circulation. He turned as if fed up and ready to leave.

"Okay, okay, sit down," Pryce said.

Brashear paused for effect, then eased into a chair across from Pryce, leaving some room so that he could move fast if necessary.

"You wanna drink, Zig-Zag?"

"Nothing. Let's deal."

"Take it easy. You're moving too fast."

"When I make a buy, that's how I do it."

"What's your sweat? Have a drink."

"I told you, I don't want no damn drink. Now look, Pryce, the only reason I'm rapping with you is because Mouse said you've got fifty caps to sell. If you do, I want them."

"Mouse has a fat mouth."

"That's her tough luck. We do business?"

"Let's see some green."

"Come off it, Pryce. I'm not flashing no wad in here any more than you're carrying the smack. You trot out the caps, and you'll be paid."

"Ten bucks per."

Brashear scraped his chair back. "H isn't that scarce."

"Wait a mo. This stuff is ten-percent pure."

"Sure it is," Brashear said caustically. "Mouse told me it was good nickel-baggings but no more than that."

"Mouse doesn't know her ass from a hole in the ground." Pryce was getting anxious now. "Look, it's better than that, honest. Eight bucks a cap."

"Six-fifty, and I take all you've got. *If* it's good."

"All?"

"You hard of hearing, Pryce? That's . . . three twenty-five, C.O.D. for fifty."

"You work it tight, don't you?"

"Do we deal?"

Pryce gnawed his lower lip, but his eyes told Brashear his mind was made up. "We deal," he said, standing up. He flexed his shoulders as if he'd somehow strained himself while slouching. "Only reason I'm letting go so cheap is that you're taking them all, you understand. That, and I've a real heavy date lined up."

"Don't worry, you'll keep your date."

Brashear watched Pryce thread his way between the small round tables, each with its spotlight and huddle of customers. Pryce went into the men's room, the door having a silhouette of a little boy pissing upright with his pants bagged around his ankles. The ladies' room door next to it had one of a girl squatting on a chamber pot. The stench from the other side of them wasn't half so funny.

Brashear turned away, peering around the cocktail lounge. The Alley Cat was at the lower end of Portlawn, hot and dark and occasionally violent. Psychedelic posters adorned the plaster walls around the tables, and the heads who weren't sitting were bellied to the bar or standing around, swacked out of their minds. The Rolling Stones were being poisoned in the jukebox, their death agonies a screaming pulse through the dismal air.

Feeding time at the zoo, Brashear thought sourly. He despised the Alley Cat, hated it the way he hated the other head shops down along the river, but he was aware that to sack this place would only start another someplace else, perhaps harder to find and control. That was the only reason he could stomach it in here; that, and knowing he was doing something about it, even if it was through compromise.

Pryce returned, holding up the dripping wet sleeve of his shirt. "Guess where I hid the stuff."

Brashear didn't bother. "If you've got it, we're going outside."

"The hell we are. I haven't finished my beer yet."

"You sure deal the hard way, Pryce. No telling who's got his eye on us in here, and I'm not about to be busted on account of your beer. We go outside where I can see what's what."

"Don't sweat the fuzz. I've got them in my pocket."

"Fine. We're going outside. Bring the beer if you're so cheap."

Pryce's eyes narrowed, his voice turning surly. "Okay, have it your way."

"I usually do."

Brashear rose and began pushing his way toward the entrance. Pryce hesitated for a last look at his Rheingold, then shoved after him, cursing under his breath. The closer to the door, the more crowded it became, people jammed shoulder-to-shoulder as though on a rush-hour bus. The front door was frosted glass set in a chrome frame, the glass painted over except for a porthole at face level. In the middle of the port was the outline of a scrawny cat, arching its back like one of those Halloween decorations, all spit and claws.

Brashear reached the door just as a drunk pushed against the cat with palm of one fat hand, fingers splayed outward. The drunk was middle-aged, moon-faced and bleary-eyed, with a nose bulbous and red-veined, and bald save for a fringe of hair like a tired, fuzzy laurel around the back of his head. His spotted tie was askew, his once-white shirt stretched over the paunch of his gut, and only one button held his flashily striped sports coat together.

Judas Cross

"Watch it, fella," the drunk said thickly, lurching into him.

"Flake off." Brashear leaned against the man, sending him stumbling out onto the sidewalk as the door opened.

"Sonsabitches, all sonsabitches," the drunk swore, moving on rubber legs toward the dark parking lot around the side.

"Who's that?" Pryce asked suspiciously from behind.

Brashear turned. Bryce's pale face had taken on a Christmas glow from the red and green neon sign overhead, giving him a sickly tan that was oddly pleasing to Brashear. "I dunno," he answered with a shrug. "Some slob who couldn't score and's going home to hump the wife, I guess."

"I don't like it." Pryce was becoming jittery in the night air.

"Man, you're something else," Brashear laughed. "It's right on when there's a thousand people around, but one lousy bum by himself sets you wetting your pants."

He started walking toward the lot, wondering if he wasn't working it too close to the bone. He didn't think Pryce was as bothered by the drunk as he was of being alone in a pitch-black alley with a man like Zig-Zag. Not that it mattered too much; he could take Pryce right here and there'd be enough, but still . . . "Tell you what," he said over his shoulder. "If it'll make you feel better, we'll deal right around the corner. No chance of anybody getting burned that way."

Pryce, tagging behind, began, "Yeah, but—"

Brashear swiveled around again, this time viciously. "Pryce, in less than a minute you'll have my money, and I'll be holding if there's any trouble. Remember that, 'cause if this deal sours, I'll know who to come looking for."

Pryce remained sullen and silent until they reached the mouth of the narrow parking lot, looking behind and about him with erratic motions of his head every few steps of the way. Then, in the shadows, he asked in a parched voice, "Where's that guy now?"

"He's left."

"No car came out."

"The other way, then, around the back."

"I didn't hear anything."

"For Christ's sake, for all I know he passed out halfway

there! You don't see him, do you? Now, come on over here by this first car, and have those caps ready."

The car was a dull-gray Ford four-door sedan, parked diagonally to the rough brick side of the building. During the day it could have been almost any color; in the dark all cars are gray. Brashear jockeyed his position so that he had a slight advantage to the entrance, Pryce with one side against the cool metal of the front fender. He unzipped his jacket and reached in with his left hand, bringing out a roll of bills which had been folded in an inside pocket. He counted out three hundred and twenty-five dollars, replaced the balance and handed the bills to Pryce. He didn't like giving the money to Pryce—there'd be hell to pay if something went wrong and Pryce got away with it—but it was necessary for the fool game, and kept Pryce's hands busy.

"Don't move until I check the stuff, Pryce."

Pryce had his eyes on the money as he unbuttoned his shirt and removed two envelopes. "It's good, I tell you. Try any cap you want; there's twenty-five in each envelope."

Brashear ripped open the first envelope and brought out a glassine packet full of fine, grayish-white powder. He opened the packet and tasted a few grains on the end of his finger. It was very bitter. There was quinine in it, but it was heroin.

"See?" Pryce said eagerly. "Good stuff, isn't it?"

"Take him, Moss," Brashear said quietly.

The drunk seemed to materialize out of nowhere, coming from the other side of the Ford and using the hood ornament as a pivot to clear the bumper, a .38 S&W Special in his hand. "Hold it," he said, "you're under arrest."

"Wha . . . ?" Pryce spun with the reaction of blind panic and hit the drunk with the full force of his arm and fist before he knew what he was doing. The drunk ran into it with the deltoid of his right shoulder, an instant of angered surprise crossing his face as the grip on his pistol went numb and he staggered backward against the car. Fear puckered Pryce as he realized he shouldn't have done that, not and stay in one piece, but then at the same time he knew he didn't want to be busted for selling heroin, which was doing a felony the hard way, and he turned to get the hell out of there while he still had a second's chance.

Judas Cross

Brashear was waiting for him. He had had his right hand inside his jacket from the moment he'd called to his partner, Moss, and he brought out his stubby Colt .38 Agent, which had been butt-forward in a Buckheimer semi-shoulder holster, and slapped Pryce across the face with it. Like brass knuckles, it ripped flesh from Pryce's cheekbone and sent him spinning against Moss, who clubbed him across the ear with the side of his fist. Pryce screamed and fell writhing to the gritty blacktop, clutching his face in both hands.

Brashear stood spread-legged, his lips pressed back over his teeth in a half grin, half grimace. "Lightfoot the Elephant to the rescue," he kidded his partner. "That was true grace, Moss."

Moss reholstered his pistol and scowled. "Somebody took a leak back there. Next time, you lie down and smell it and see how fresh you are."

"Next time, go easier on the drunk act. Pryce got leery."

"Who was acting? Jesus, I had five gins waiting for you to make your move. I thought you'd gone to sleep, you took so long." He buttoned his jacket, looking down at the peddler with disdain. "Name's Pryce, huh? All right, get up, Pryce. Come on, you're not hurt bad."

Pryce moaned, trying to get his legs under him. "Goddamn, I've been paying right along, paying all you cops. Why're you doing this to me?"

Crimson blotches pulsed on Moss's temples. He hated the mention of payoffs, and he hated it worse when it came from a creep like Pryce. They didn't call Mossam Turnbeau "the Monk" for nothing. He reached down and grabbed the front of Pryce's shirt, jamming him upright against the car. "Don't say cops take bribes, shitheel. Don't make it worse for you than it is. Now turn around and place your hands against the roof."

Pryce leaned against the car, blood from his cheek dripping along the side of the door. "I ain't carrying no gun."

"Shut up." Moss Turnbeau patted him down more roughly than he had to, not finding any weapons but coming up with a wallet and a flat, soot-blackened tin box from his pants pockets. The tin had once held English cigarettes; now it contained an eyedropper, a needle and a couple of wads of cotton. "Looky here, a layout," he said, passing the wallet and tin to his partner.

Brashear flipped through the wallet. "Says here you're from Passaic, George," he said, using Pryce's first name. "That so?"

Pryce didn't reply, only sniffing loudly to clear his nose.

"You got a record, George?"

Pryce remained silent.

"Here or the station, Georgie boy. Suit yourself."

Pryce said, "I don't have to answer nothing. I know my rights."

"Tell him his rights, Moss," Brashear said.

"In keeping with the Supreme Court decision in Miranda versus Arizona, I'm advising you that you may remain silent and not answer any police questions but if you do your answers may be used as evidence against you and that you may consult an attorney before or during police questioning and if you don't have the funds to hire counsel you are entitled to have a lawyer appointed without cost." He droned the words together in a single breath. "Clear?"

"I wanna lawyer."

"You understand your rights?" Turnbeau persisted.

"Yeah, yeah, I unnerstand them."

"No, you don't," Turnbeau said, and punched him in the kidney.

Pryce screamed. But that was all right because this was down by the river, and down by the river lots of screaming went on that went ignored.

"Where the hell you think you are?" Turnbeau shouted at him. "You're in Portlawn, New Jersey, that's where you are, a pimple on my ass, and I'll squeeze you as hard as I want."

"Let's see your arms, George," Brashear said.

Pryce was whimpering, but he slowly turned to face them, wavering on his feet as he fumbled with his cuffs.

"Jesus, hurry it up!" Turnbeau's face was beet-red now.

Pryce managed to bare his arms. The insides of his elbows were dotted with punctures, the skin puffy and purplish yellow.

"More chicken tracks than in a hen coop," Brashear said. "How long you been a hype, George?"

"I dunno what you mean. I must've scratched myself."

Judas Cross

"Knock it off. How long?"

"I did some chipping once, but that was years ago."

"Stop shitting us, George. Those tracks haven't even started to heal yet."

"Infected, too," Turnbeau said. "Don't you know enough to clean your needle first, Pryce?"

"So *okay!* So I shoot sometimes. So big deal."

"Moving up in the world, aren't you?" Turnbeau asked.

"What d'you mean?"

"The caps, Georgie. Where'd a hype like you get fifty caps?" Brashear demanded. "You're pushing for somebody else. Who?"

"You've got it wrong. I've been saving them up."

"Not on your habit, you haven't. Must be three a day at least."

"I've been saving them, little at a time when the price has been right, and that's the way it sticks. You got me and I'll do some time, but you just try and prove I didn't save them up."

"Lots of time, George, especially if you're uncooperative. That the way you want us to put it down? Uncooperative?"

"Jesus, I can't stand any more," Turnbeau said. "Let's take him in."

"Fine by me." Brashear squatted to scoop up the money that had scattered when Pryce fell. "You call in. I want to go back and get some cigarettes." He placed the money and envelopes on the front seat of the Ford while his partner cuffed Pryce with his hands behind his back, then he opened the back door and stood holding it, grinning.

"Mother," Pryce swore as he was hustled inside. "You're both mothers, busting me like this. I paid my grease. I should've been left alone."

"Yeah, but you forgot one thing, George."

"What?"

"You didn't buy us. You couldn't."

The last word, and Brashear strode off toward the Alley Cat entrance feeling very bullish. He felt bullish because he was a "bull"—Detective 3rd/grade Daniel Junius Brashear, as contrasted to being a patrolman in harness. He felt bullish because he took pride in his work—that gritty, bittersweet kind of pride which is a policeman's compromise between the necessity of being around garbage like Pryce and the satisfaction of removing it from his city's streets.

Dammit, he was *doing* something about it, and nobody could take that pleasure from him. Not his father, once a cop himself but resisting his son's following the paternal footsteps with the passion of a man wishing better things for his offspring. Nor his old college professors, stagnating in verbiage and calcifying in theories, who considered the police to have the intelligence of a frog pond, yet whose peeks at reality came only from campus riots. Not even his wife could . . . but that was unfair. Valerie's objections were to his beard and smell, his disguise an anathema to her. You couldn't blame her.

Brashear went through the swinging door, back into the pure shriek of the Alley Cat. He cut through the crowd with his shoulders until he reached the far end of the bar, next to the cigarette machine. He waited until Kirby, the head bartender, could break free, dropping a couple of quarters into the machine for Chesterfield Kings.

Kirby was a stocky man with pale eyes dulled from smoke and dimness, and an iron-gray mustache that drooped over his mouth, successfully hiding any expression. He came over, nervously wiping his hands on his apron as he always did. "Make it simple," he said. "One man off, and it's been hell tonight."

"Short Coke. Got to remember my breath."

"Uh-huh." Kirby went away, serving a few drinks and ringing up the cash register a couple of times before returning with Brashear's Coke. He placed a half-filled Tom Collins glass on a paper doily, then leaned against the back wall and dried his hands some more. "Everything go all right?"

"No trouble."

"I'll lose my license if any more arrests happen in here."

"Don't worry, not this one. We bagged him in the street."

Kirby nodded as if relieved. "There was a guy in here."

"A guy? What guy?"

"Never saw him before last night. One of those suit-and-starch prim ones, y'know?"

Judas Cross

"Well, what about him?"

"He was asking a lot of questions. Ordered a sherry, would you believe, and tried to pump us." Kirby's dull eyes gazed at Brashear's glass and doily. "I didn't say anything, though."

"Why, Kirby, what's there to tell?"

"Go ahead and grin, he could have been from this new committee. This Wilcox thing, sniffing around for their investigation."

"You must drink lots of milk."

"What makes you say that?" Kirby asked, glancing up.

"Worry. You're always worrying, and that gets the acid going. For Christ's sake, how many of these probes have you seen come and go since you've been here, Kirby? A dozen maybe, and I bet you've got an ulcer from each one. So what if this guy was from the Wilcox Committee? It's only politics; don't mean a thing to us."

"Glad you're so sure."

"Go drink some milk, Kirby."

"I would if there was time." Kirby sighed, moving away from the wall. "About tonight. The Alley Cat's clear, isn't it?"

"I said it was. I'll even write the report myself."

"Your partner still got a hard-on about things like this?"

"That's not nice," Brashear said evenly.

"Sure," Kirby said, backing. "Sure . . . and thanks."

Brashear watched Kirby return to tending bar, and shook his head ruefully at the jittery nerves the man displayed. Kirby belonged someplace quieter where the action was less corrosive, someplace like his own neighborhood, which was a pretty nice area of Portlawn to live and raise a family. He slid the Coke off the doily, idly wondering if Kirby would ever get the gumption to quit and look around. In a way he hoped not; then there'd be the problem of breaking in a new man here, which was always risky.

Underneath the doily were two folded ten-dollar bills, payment for having arrested Pryce away from the Alley Cat. Brashear pocketed the twenty and downed the free Coke in three swallows.

There were all sorts of compromises you made being a cop.

1-b

Breezes of early September glided with the Sanponset, swiftly circling downward as the river flowed over the falls in the middle of Portlawn, then swirling upward again in tight spirals of chill, forecasting the coming months. Promises written in summer sun and bolt ends of dreams spun under August moon were sent spinning through the darkened streets of the Falls District precinct, dying with the season, fading as the nights grew longer. And like the wind, the men of the Falls District precinct were thin, cool influences on the 66,000 inhabitants of its area, ignored or endured depending on the thickness of protection, the cost of insulation.

Brashear was one of the men of the Falls District. He had been since his graduation from Fairleigh Dickinson University, and an especially nasty row with his father afterward in the campus parking lot. The particular of the argument had been over his refusing a trainee position with Oldsmobile; the general had been as always, a theme recurring like a chorus from Gilbert and Sullivan: *A policeman's lot is not a happy one.*

"You weren't sent through college to become a flatfoot like me . . ." No, but that's what I've always wanted to become, Dad. Not like childhood cowboy and rocketship dreams, but because of what you've been to me as a father and as a man. Don't you see? Can't you be proud . . . ? "I never had your chances, so don't waste yours . . ." What good are chances if I can't make my choice from them? College was your insistence, not mine . . . "If you're too blind to think of your own future, consider Valerie's. She's your wife, son . . ." Through deceit. Pleasant deceit, for I love her and would have married her anyway, but deceit nevertheless. She quite literally made her own bed, and she'll have to lie in it as best she can . . .

It had been a lopsided fight, the outspoken bluster of one against the hidden thoughts of the other, until finally the pain and resentment had overwhelmed Dan Brashear and he'd torn off his mortarboard and stomped it into the gravel. He'd refused to return to upstate New York with his parents, knowing with

Judas Cross

anguish he would never join his father's force. But nearby Portlawn was recruiting; Brashear had gone there searching for a new home.

For six years now, home had been a somber quarter block of stone and concrete at the corner of Fourth and Harrison. It was a Gay Nineties pomposity, built when public architecture was supposed to be imposing and enduring as religion, four blocks from the waterfall which gave the district its name, and overlooking a flat, dull-brown park. Five of the six years had been lived on the ground floor, a patrolman under Captain Batavia. The last eight months had been upstairs in the Detective Division, where he was one of twelve assigned to Lieutenant Jules. He was doing what he wanted to do, and well enough to rise fast and smooth. In due course he'd become 2nd/grade, and then after that . . .

Well, there was a lot for Brashear to feel bullish about.

He would have felt prouder if it weren't for the motto over the front door of his home. The station entrance was up three broad steps and through a stilted archway, two Florentine bracket lamps like giant dungeon torches on either side of the arch's springing line. Above the keystone was an escutcheon with a motto around its rim reading JVSTITIA HONORIS PRAEMIVM, "Justice is the reward of honor." The escutcheon was made of small, hand-hewn granite bricks, and ever since he'd worn the lint off his first uniform, Brashear had the oddly nagging idea that one day, one of those bricks was going to dislodge and hit him.

There it was. A patina of grime had dimmed its already faint outline to almost a pattern of shadows in the light of the lamps' frosted globes. The individual letters of the motto were black streaks cemented together, and damned if that *H* didn't seem to stand out as if loose. Brashear gripped Pryce's bent arm and shoved the man through the arch, vexed by this absurdity which gnawed at him.

What was provoking it? Not the trouble with his father, surely. That, thank God, had mellowed over the years, especially with the birth of Lisa. Parents can be very forgiving when they become grandparents, not that there was anything to forgive.

Though there was still a matter of his old mortarboard. His father had it prominently displayed on a bookcase, mashed and battered like a souvenir a soldier would bring back from the wars.

His marriage was solid, the kid healthy. Whatever it was had nothing to do with Valerie or Lisa, he could tell that much.

No problems at the station, either. He went out of his way to get along with the guys, to be a "regular," and knew that his promotion was mostly the result of having kept his nose clean, with nothing against him either on his record or among the men. He readily conformed to the traditions of the department, right down to the Alley Cat's twenty bucks in his pocket. Make that twenty-five—he'd picked up a fin that afternoon for ignoring the dust clouds and double-parked trucks of a construction outfit. But, hell, everybody did things like that; it was *expected* of you.

Still vaguely dissatisfied, Brashear thrust Pryce ahead of him, through the squeaky double doors and into the muster room.

Fratelli was desk sergeant. His well-veined face was lowered as he studiously read *Three's a Sandwich*, a dog-eared paperback that had been making the rounds since it'd been pinched from the back pocket of a young suspect two weeks before. Fratelli had been on the force longer than Turnbeau, longer than almost anybody, a monument to the stoic passage to retirement.

" 'Lo, Andy," Turnbeau said to him.

"Yo," Fratelli said, looking up. He always said "Yo," just as he always was reading, his lips forming each word carefully.

"Check us in, will you?"

"Glad to." Fratelli didn't have to check in detectives, but it was part of the ritual when he was holding down the desk. Almost a tradition considering his tenure, and it made him feel needed, now that he was pretty much out of things. Writing in the log, he said, "Quiet night. Most that's happened is Robard getting sick. Said it was probably something he had for dinner."

"Bet it was the coffee he makes. Who's catching instead?"

"Carberry."

Judas Cross

Brashear turned to Pryce, a slow grin on his face. "You'll like Carberry, George."

"Fuck you, whatever your name is," Pryce said.

"His name's Zig-Zag," Turnbeau told him. "Didn't he tell you?"

"Fuck you too, you bald-headed bastard."

"Somehow the English language loses its charm when it is reduced to a constant barrage of four-letter words," Fratelli said, deadpan. "There are no longer any nuances, don't you think?"

Fratelli could string obscenities together better than anybody. His philosophy was good for a laugh from Brashear as Turnbeau propelled Pryce toward the stairs at the far side of the muster room. The Detective Division was on the third floor, a flight above a mezzanine for clerks and secretaries, and though there was an elevator of sorts, the stairs were always used for prisoners and suspects. Helped break their will, staggering as they did up the steps, off balance with their hands behind them.

Brashear watched his partner ahead and could almost feel Turnbeau's joints aching. After fifteen years of pounding one kind of pavement or another, they couldn't help but creak some, but that's a perfect example of what happens when you try to buck the system. Only reason Moss wasn't still in uniform was because of a bit of heroism eight years before which had gained lots of publicity and a generous kick upstairs. Moss was a good cop, a damn good cop, but the third floor would be as high as he'd ever get. Trouble was he never took an extra anything, not even a free cup of coffee, and while he never ratted on those who did, it went against the grain. The Monk. Brashear wondered peripherally if Moss knew his nickname, and figured he must by this time. He wasn't dumb, he knew the score; what Brashear couldn't understand was why Moss had never bent.

Portlawn was run loose, from the mayor on down. There was some gambling and numbers, a few roundheels plying their trade, a tolerance on bar hours, but it was kept local and none of it was heavy. Drug peddling, organized prostitution, shakedowns, sex deviations—that stuff was hit and hit hard, no bribes interfering. Witness tonight: Pryce was one thing, the Alley Cat another. It had to be that way, or they'd enforce so many unwanted laws that the real work would never get done. Buying some blind eye was for Portlawn's own good, whether the residents knew it or not.

Besides, even as a detective Brashear earned only $7,420. After insurance deductions, federal and real-estate taxes, precinct bed tax, and benevolent fund, he was lucky to clear $215 every first and fifteenth. Try raising a family and buying a house, and you'd see how fast an extra $200 or so a month helped out. Valerie understood, that was something. Some of the guys couldn't tell their wives about their extra income, but not with Valerie. She understood how a city had to be run, how a cop never got ahead unless he went along with the system. And she sure liked the finer things. As she said, it was only sensible and certainly nothing to be ashamed of.

So why the feeling about the motto? He didn't know . . .

The Detective Division was just to the right of the top of the stairs. Across the stippled glass door was painted, logically enough, DETECTIVE DIVISION in block capitals, and down near the doorknob was ENTER HERE. The division itself was a rectangular room, the floor and wainscot done in dark wood strips, and the rest of the wall and the ceiling painted an innocuous beige. There was a slatted railing just inside the door to keep the natives at bay, and on the other side was a row of chewed-up desks alongside screened windows. In one corner was a yellowed sink and a medicine cabinet filled with bottles and cups, then a string of filing cabinets ending at the inner door to Lieutenant Jules's office. The opposite wall had a flat table against it, and a cage. The cage was six feet square, wrought iron grilled from floor to ceiling like an old-fashioned elevator shaft. There was a chair inside it, and a sign hanging on the open door reminded you that it should be locked when used.

Home. Brashear's home, with the smell of most police rooms; that saccharine sourness of blood, sweat and tears.

Detective 2nd/grade Carberry sat at one of the desks, his jacket around the hard-backed chair. He weighed two hundred pounds but was only five-eight, which accounted for the bulge of

Judas Cross

his biceps as he pecked at an ancient Underwood, and for the thick line of his jaw as he clamped down on a cigar. The cigar was small and cheap, with a plastic tip; it was the only kind he could scavenge free in large quantities and still have it withstand his teeth. He was known to chew suspects with the same crude zeal.

"Look what dragged in," he said as the three entered.

"Heard Robard couldn't stomach your B.O. any longer and went home," Turnbeau responded. He opened the gate in the railing, swinging it wide for Pryce and Brashear. "A regular fiend for baths, aren't you, Ed?"

Carberry went, "Ha ha."

Brashear glanced at the empty cage. "Where's the boy?"

"Williams? The security dick from Granite Brothers, Marty Fatt, took him to dinner."

"To *dinner*? Marty Fatt never picked up a tab in his life."

"He is this time. Who've you got there?"

"George Pryce, possession with intent to sell. So far." Brashear steered Pryce to the cage and locked him inside. "Since Williams is out, we'll let George stew here awhile, think things over."

"Won't admit he's even in Jersey," Turnbeau said. "But give him time, give him time."

Pryce gripped the bars, glaring between them at Brashear. "Think you're real smart, don't you?"

"You figure it out. I'm not the one facing ten at Trenton."

"Blow it out your ass, it'll never happen."

"He's a cutie," Carberry said, beginning to grin. "He's a cutie. He lips off to me, and his ass'll be grass."

Turnbeau was dumping the envelopes of heroin, evidence money and Pryce's layout on the desk behind Carberry. "You got any extra Complaint Report blanks, Ed? I'm fresh out."

"Yeah, but you can forget it for now. You and Dan are to relieve Schmidt and Nalisco. They're staked in unit Twelve of the Bideewee Motel, out on Laurentide."

"Ed, you know how we hate horning in on true love."

Carberry looked at Turnbeau's mock-serious expression and chose to ignore it. "The unit's registered to a John Quaker of

Baltimore, only the manager hasn't seen him or his car in ten days. Some dame named Irene . . ." He paused to run a thumb down a pad beside the typewriter. "Irene Jeliknek, if that isn't a hell of a name, has been staying there with him, paying the bills. Tonight she took a knife to her wrists—maybe. She was in too bad a shape, when found, to give a story."

"He ditched her and she tried a dutch. So why the maybe?"

"Some of Quaker's stuff is still in the room, Dan, including a Ruger Blackhawk .41 Magnum. Now, a dame's just a dame, but no man's going to run out on sweet hardware like that."

"True, true."

"The loot thinks it's worth waiting to see if this Quaker returns, or until his pussy can explain what happened and why the Ruger."

"The girl going to make it?"

Carberry shrugged. "Last report I got is that she's in Intensive, but mostly due to loss of blood. She should."

Turnbeau shook his head, scratching his forehead. "Jesus, Ed, I've got a ton of paper work, and—"

"I weep. Orders is orders, so get out there and don't fall asleep. Pryce can molt there; we're booking Williams later."

"He finally confess?"

"Not exactly. You know, three days now Fatt and the day crew haven't budged him, the little stinker insisting he deposited the receipts in Mideastern like he was supposed to. Fatt finally got so pissed off he told the kid Granite was pressing charges unless they got their money back, and wasn't it worth fifteen hundred dollars just to get out of the mess. Which is a crock of shit, but the kid don't know and he says yes, maybe his parents will loan it to him. Then Fatt reels him in, saying Granite needs a statement to close the records, and getting the money from the parents won't do. How about a story that Williams can't remember what happened that night after he left the store? No explanation where the money was, no confession he took it; just a blackout that'll please everybody."

"For Christ's sake, the kid fell for it?" Brashear snapped. "Nobody told him that statement's what's needed to arrest him?"

Judas Cross

"Hell, no. What for? Fatt caps it by saying, 'Son, you do this, and I'll take you to dinner, just to prove there's no hard feelings.' What the hell, Williams was one hard nut to crack, he had to be tricked."

"Come on, I saw him. He's all of nineteen and scared green. He could be telling the truth. Maybe the bank screwed up and lost the deposit; you know as well as I do that Mideastern's security is as tight as a crab net. Remember the teller who skipped to England?"

"So what? Williams is from Seattle or someplace far off like that there. Mideastern's here in Portlawn, and so is Granite, and they're the ones we have to live with. Who wants to stir up trouble when we've got a strong case already?"

"Because it's a crappy thing to do, that's why! You're ruining a kid's future on a phony confession that's illegal besides!"

"Don't yell at me, Brashear. More'n likely the kid's guilty, and if he ain't, he's probably guilty of something else."

Brashear looked away, his bullishness gone, evaporated in the heat of sudden anger. *Jvstitia Honoris Praemivm*—maybe Carberry is right and it's justice. But it surely wasn't honorable. "Does Williams know he needs a lawyer yet?" he snarled. "No, I bet."

"We'll likely get him Longacre when he does."

"Longacre! Longacre would steal the blanket out of his mother's kennel! Williams doesn't have a chance with Longacre!"

Carberry shrugged, supremely unconcerned.

From the cage came a derisive snort: "Jersey justice."

Brashear pivoted, snapping with frustrated viciousness, "Shut up, Pryce, you'll be getting your share of it soon enough."

Carberry belched, covering it politely with the hand holding his cigar.

Brashear swallowed thickly, his throat full of cotton as he wondered about himself. His sudden flare-up confused him, becoming more obscure and yet at the same time deeper as he realized that he was reacting irrationally now to more than just the motto. He tried to think of an answer to Carberry, but not even clichés came to mind, unable as he was to finger the reason for the resentment he had caused between them. He felt frustrated, so damn *stupid*.

Turnbeau spoke after a moment, calmly and distinctly as if choosing his words. "Come on, Dan. We've got to relieve the stake."

Brashear nodded and turned toward the door. He was harassed by his abrupt lack of control, impatient with himself, and the skin of his neck crawled from knowing Carberry was staring at his back, wondering. But Carberry wasn't looking at all; as the door shut he was negligently blowing smoke rings at one of the meshed lamp fixtures in the ceiling . . .

Going down the stairs, Turnbeau worriedly watched his partner. He wasn't sure he could have stopped the outburst, or more important, if he'd wanted to, but Brashear seemed to have withdrawn into his own private world because of it. His body was rigid, hands punched in his pockets, bearded face shadowed by the poor light of the stairwell but pale nonetheless. When they reached the mezzanine Turnbeau paused, his right hand fumbling with the button of his jacket, his mind groping for a way into Brashear's thoughts.

"Dan—"

"No, don't," Brashear said sharply. "I shouldn't have sounded off back there and I know it. Don't say anything and make it worse."

They remained silent the rest of the way down. Every few seconds, though, Turnbeau studied Brashear with concerned and puzzled intensity. He thought Brashear would pass Fratelli without the usual parting routine, but Brashear surprised him.

" 'Night, Andy," Brashear said. "Sign us out, will you?" Then he stopped, one palm rubbing his thick black hair. "Say, Andy, do you remember an old cartoon strip where a cat was always being hit with a brick when he wasn't expecting it?"

Fratelli laid his book aside. "Yeah, Ignatz the Cat, I think."

"It was Krazy Kat," Turnbeau said. "Ignatz was the mouse who threw the bricks. Trouble with you, Andy, you got no culture."

Fratelli's ears reddened. "It was Ignatz," he said stubbornly, and then, sensing the corner Turnbeau could put him in, turned on Brashear. "What difference is it? Why did you ask, anyway?"

Brashear stood with his head cocked to one side, frowning, his eyes wandering a little. "Forget it, Andy," he said in a low, bewildered voice. "It doesn't matter. Doesn't matter at all."

1-c

Laurentide Avenue is a scalpel, incising Interstate 80 and dissecting the heart of downtown Portlawn northward to routes 4, 20 and 208. During the day it drains the blood of business to Fair Lawn, Paramus, Ridgewood, and a dozen other suburban cancers not quite malignant enough to be terminal.

But with the night, Laurentide becomes a motorized carnival for a million cars. Back and forth, in and about, going nowhere but going impatiently; the drum of engines erratic to the rhythm of stop lights; the sway of passengers excitative to the flow of congestion; the acid rock from eight-track stereos a throbbing pulse like calliopes thumping out the beat. Around them the side-show vendors simper and the midway barkers wink—choose, don't browse; buy, don't touch. And overhead the pungent fumes of exhaust hang like the breath from a clockwork monster.

Just back of the lights and noise, in the quiet shadows of shrubbery and flagstone, are the motels like a row of plaster sausages on a neon string. The ones nearest Interstate 80 have color TV and organists in their lounges, but the closer you get to Portlawn, the older and cheaper they become, ending in crackerbox specials at five dollars a night or two dollars an hour, an all-night maid running ragged changing sheets. In the middle are the "commercials": Spartan and clean, existing on businessmen's discounts and managed by couples who live in back of the office and unplug the switchboard at 11 P.M.

The Bideewee was one of the middle kind, with another unpretentious motel on one side and a diner on the other. It was L-shaped, two-storied, with an outside balcony connecting the upper rooms, its rear wing extending behind the diner and encircled by a looping driveway. Unit 12 was at one end of the ground-floor rear wing, on the side facing away from Laurentide. Schmidt and Nalisco's unmarked cruiser was parked in a vacant slot around front, so as not to draw suspicion from Quaker should he return, but Nalisco was behind the wheel, smoking a cigarette when Brashear and Turnbeau drove up. He signaled to them, flipping the cigarette out the window.

Nalisco was a thin blond man in his late thirties who looked to be made of steel cord and could make it seem that way in a scuffle. He was dressed in plain clothes, as they all were, and standing in the driveway, he hitched his pants and said, "I was going nuts in there. No lights, no television, no smoking, no nothing."

Turnbeau turned to him with disgust. "You mean all you do is sit there?"

"You better believe it. Schmidt's been in the same chair since we started, arms folded and legs braced apart, you know how he is. A goddamn stone bird dog, pointing at the door. That I could stand, but he keeps asking me about the qualifying test he's taking next week. What's it like? What are the questions about? A guy can take just so much of that. I had to get out for a smoke."

They were walking around the side of the rear wing now, almost to unit 12. "And if Quaker showed?" Brashear asked.

"Ah, he's not coming. The looie's got a fig up his butt over nothing. I think Carberry got Jules all excited just so he could act big man while catching for Robard. You heard Robard is sick, didn't you?" Nalisco rapped sharply on the end door, its only distinguishing mark the brass numerals 12 near the top.

The latch snapped back after a moment and Schmidt opened the door. He was of average height and build, with bush-cut salt-and-pepper hair, jowls and basset eyes. "So, about time," he said, and paused to eye Turnbeau speculatively. Then: "Moss, friend to friend, where the hell did you get that jacket?"

Turnbeau glanced down at his coat, puzzled. "What d'you mean?"

"Those colors, those stripes. The other one was worn out, I

Judas Cross

know, but this . . . To keep down your age you wear it, maybe?"

"It hides his liver spots," Nalisco said.

"There's nothing wrong with my coat! I like it fine."

"You would," Nalisco said.

"Me, I'd burn it." Schmidt stepped out onto the narrow sidewalk, beckoning toward the darkened room. "Have fun, boys."

"Listen, I talked to the manager earlier," Nalisco said, "and she's agreed to watch television in the office out front. If Quaker does show up, she'll ring the room real quick. You want to grab a quick cup of coffee or something at the diner, do it before the end of Johnny Carson."

"You catch Quaker," Schmidt added, "and I've got dibs on his Ruger."

"We flipped a coin for it," Nalisco explained.

"Let me guess," Brashear said, going inside. "Loser takes the gold fillings as consolation. Christ, it's black in here."

"Not with Moss' sports coat, it isn't. You better hide it, Moss, or they'll think the lights are on."

"Very funny. How'd you know which side the coin landed?" Turnbeau said. "Kiss it?"

"No need," Schmidt replied. "I used my two-headed nickel."

"Abe has all the luck," Nalisco said and shut the door on a sharp bark of laughter.

Turnbeau stared at the door malevolently. "If Quaker was out there, those two clowns chased him away for sure. What a way to run a stakeout."

Brashear glanced around, his eyes gradually becoming accustomed to the dimness. He sensed a loneliness to the room, as if he and Turnbeau weren't really there; an isolation common to most hotel or motel rooms, no matter how long they've been occupied. "Nalisco's probably right, though," he said. "A waste of time."

"It better not be, or I'll kick Carberry's fat ass for sure. Jesus, there's nothing I hate worse than sitting in the hole like this."

"One good thing."

"Cheer me."

"We're not with Pryce. Wait until that hype starts coming down screaming for another fix. Carberry will really suffer."

"Not as much as Pryce will." Turnbeau settled in one of the room's two chairs, hoisting his brogues on the bed. "Sit down, Dan."

But Brashear was too jumpy to relax. His sudden rage had calmed since leaving the station, but there was an unexplainable residue from it which was making him feel frustrated and irritable. It was more than the Williams case, he could sense that much. The boy was not his responsibility; he dealt with enough agony in his own work without contemplating another's. You had to stay detached and objective to do the job properly, like a good executioner. Brashear had been taught this, believed this, and had always considered himself to be doing this. Yet his chronic aggravation by the motto, and tonight his outburst at Carberry, preyed on his mind now, leaving him confused and restive.

There was nothing in the motel room to divert him, either, other than the shadowy glow from the curtained window and the ghostly dishevel of the unmade bed and disordered furniture. He paced in moody inspection, intent more on ignoring his own disorder than the room's.

This woman, this Irene Jeliknek; she seemed to have been relatively tidy as compared to most shack-up jobs he'd investigated. There was the scent of steamy clothes, of passion gone but not forgotten, but the bureau and bedstands weren't cluttered, and things weren't strewn all over the floor. Only blood, quantities of it, in great black stains trailing from the bathroom across the carpet. That's the way it so often is, he thought. Hesitation marks over the sink because she was a neat person, a determined final slicing with her eyes closed, or perhaps staring tormentedly at her reflection in the cabinet mirror. Then the spurt of crimson panic, the hysteria of knowing what she'd done but not wanting to die, not really, only escape the intolerable. Brashear's eyes followed her liquid cry for help from the shiny tiles to the door, seeing the ebon smear around the knob, the staining grip on the sill . . .

No, this was impossible. He couldn't think about her; she

Judas Cross

was no more his affair than Williams was. He and Moss were only filling in on the off chance that the heel with the fancy gun would return, and in a little while they'd be working on something else. Something else. He had to think of something else, do something else.

Brashear glanced at his wrist watch, wondering how he was going to pass the tedious hours ahead. He looked across the bed at his partner, but Turnbeau was hidden in thick gloom, as if a black hood had been molded over his face. Brashear sensed he was being watched, though, just as he had felt Carberry staring at his back. What's going on in *his* mind? he asked himself, beginning to feel more nervous and depressed than ever.

"What're you thinking, Moss?"

"Me? Nothing in particular."

"About what happened here?"

"Not especially."

"What, then?" His voice sounded unnaturally urgent even to himself. "My blowup back at the station?"

"It's got you bugged, doesn't it?" Turnbeau shifted in his chair before he spoke again. Brashear considered it a hesitation, that Moss was unfinished, but it was too long a hesitation to be casual and he braced himself.

"I don't want to hear about it."

"You asked, Dan."

"Only to shut you up."

Turnbeau refused to shut up. "Look, we've been together almost since you were promoted, right? You think I'm blind? You think I haven't noticed you cringe whenever we go in the station, as if a tiger were on the roof ready to pounce? God knows why; you've bottled your emotions so tight I doubt *you* even know—but tonight the pressure was too great and some of the steam escaped."

"Stop it, Moss."

"We're a lot alike, Dan, and I believe I understand. You can't be a cop and not a cop at the same time."

"Is that what you think? I'm some sort of half a cop?"

"Well, that's one way of putting it. More a matter you're finding out the respect a cop must have—from others, from himself—is no longer given with the badge. It has to be earned."

Savagely: "So now I don't respect myself. Horsecock!"

"You know the answer better than I. All I'm saying is that to be respected you have to be respectable first, all the way through."

"You stole that line from Wilcox. Read it in the paper last week."

"Guess I did at that. But he's right, Dan."

"You hand me a pain, you and Holy Joe Wilcox and his do-good committee." Venom rose in Brashear's throat like sudden vomit, spewing out of its own volition. "You'd like to see them get to power, I suppose, and clean up the county like they've promised. Let me tell you, if do-gooders ever did, nothing would get done. Everybody would be too busy making sure the other guy didn't have his palm out to make decisions, and about the time industry moved out and the sewers backed up, the average slob would be sick of having Sunday seven times a week. Only by then our people would've been closed, and there'd be nothing to fill the vacuum except the mobs. And when the mobs get in, so do the hard drugs, the organized prostitution, corrupt unions, strong-arm and shakedown rackets. Not that I'm worried about Wilcox. I've always been suspicious of any man so pure his shit don't stink."

"Don't try changing the subject, Dan, it won't work. You—"

"I'm not! If I were the mobs, I'd contribute to Wilcox's war chest whether he was Jesus or just another hog rooting at the trough. There's no organization, no Mafia in Portlawn now, and not because they haven't tried. When they've cut in, the locals we protect have bitched and we've rousted them out, not always by the book. Sure, it's a compromise, but it works. It keeps things moving and the mobs out, and what you call being half a cop is nothing of the sort. It's being realistic. That's all police work is—a realistic compromise. Grow up, Moss, face facts."

"Most of life is a compromise to one degree or another, but you can't compromise yourself. Take Carberry—he's only half, but without the other half to know any better. He's your compromise, Dan, and you couldn't swallow it. All your fancy

Judas Cross

logic is so much bushwah at heart, so many excuses instead of reasons, and you can't fool me and you can't fool yourself with them, not deep down."

Shut up, shut the hell up! Brashear wanted to yell. He gritted his teeth instead and glared at the darkness which was speaking.

"Times have changed, Dan. Men like Carberry are out of it, because if the old compromises ever did work, they don't any more. It's the age of extremes now, of sides and no middles, and you either become like Marty Fatt to survive—a sellout, worse than the scum we handle—or a cop, a *whole* cop."

"Get off my back, you righteous bastard."

"Yeah, I'm the Monk, and you don't have to rub it in. A long time ago I had to come to terms with myself, and it was hell. It still is." Turnbeau sounded weary, slightly discouraged. "You're discovering, as I did, Dan, that you can't be just a little pregnant."

That was it, the last straw he could take. Brashear went for the door almost brutally, desperate to get out from under Turnbeau's grinding piety.

"Where're you going?"

"Out for coffee," Brashear said, his voice tightening. "To hell with it not being allowed, I'm going. You want your compromise black or regular?"

"Nothing," Turnbeau answered softly.

Brashear snapped the door shut behind him, his clenched face set against the driveway's feeble illumination. His eyes darted around in a painful, searching manner, as though he were afraid that on top of everything else, Quaker was hiding someplace close by. The night was brisk now, sharp with a cutting breeze; but without a moon. Not even a backyard window was lit to help; beyond the row of parked cars was a black misshapen phalanx. Anything could be out there and probably was. Well, to hell with that, too.

He lowered his head and began walking rapidly around the side of the building. There was a chain-link fence between the rear wing and the diner, forcing him to go all the way around and down the drive; petulantly he kicked a stone from his path, the sound of nearby Laurentide Avenue like the hum of a vast, luminous insect to his ears.

Christ, he knew he'd always had a temper, but this was absurd. Anger and resentment, rekindled from the embers of his argument with Carberry, seethed inside him, blurring individual thoughts with livid heat. He needed that cup of coffee and a chance to sit alone, calm down, sort things out. A drink would have been better, a nice fat shot of Fleischmann's rye to mellow his gut, but going to the diner was chancy enough. Thank God Nalisco had cooked up a deal with the motel manager, he thought, peering at the office as he passed beneath the entrance canopy. He smiled, relieved when he saw that the lights were on and the heavy face of a chunky, gray-haired woman was staring stupefied at a television behind the counter. Five, ten minutes and he'd be back, and he'd take a container of coffee to Turnbeau anyway, just to show there were no hard feelings. Yeah, and maybe a maple bar too . . .

When he reached the sidewalk, Brashear automatically glanced in both directions before heading for the diner. He paused—then paused again, and all thoughts of coffee suddenly vanished.

A cab was pulling away from the curb of the motel next door, after having deposited a woman on the sidewalk. She stood there, her beige cloth coat unbuttoned while she momentarily adjusted a cheap, shiny black dress the way a woman will after a ride—hands smoothing down the material over stockinged legs, head tilted so that bleached hair fell around a slender, almost prim face.

Brashear recognized the woman immediately. Out of perversity and obstinacy, as if he were compelled to prove something to himself, he moved quickly toward her. She heard his approach and looked up, tossing her hair back with a throw of her head.

"Hello, Laura," he said.

"You again. Where the hell did you come from, anyway?"

"I was having coffee in the diner when I saw you," he lied.

Judas Cross

"Just my luck. This is the second time in a week."

Brashear grinned at her. She had no last name, just Laura of a thousand beds. High-grade vulgarity, all lure, all take and no give, and he doubted that she could recall how many pay checks and expense accounts she'd squeezed dry between her transient thighs.

"How're tricks?"

"You've got it wrong. I live here."

"Then you won't mind if we talk to the manager, will you?"

She looked at him with bleak indifference, the whore's look.

He said, "A nice, private business conference, right? That should be good for a hundred, plus cab fare."

"Fifty, you sonofabitch. Things are rotten, so many amateurs."

"Uh-huh. A hundred, Laura, and it'll be ten percent."

"Have a heart. I haven't got paid yet."

"I hear Judge Cordell is a merciful man when sentencing."

Laura let out a deep sigh, knowing it was useless to argue. Part of the cost of the trade, just like her man was, though her man would probably beat her when she got back ten dollars short. He always thought she was holding out, which was true about half the time. But at least it was better than the pigs snatching you off the street and then perjuring in court that you'd grabbed their honk, which was what they did to strangers trying to work Portlawn. You got something for your money, anyway.

She opened the bag which hung from her shoulder, reaching in for her change purse. Brashear watched her, wondering slyly what Turnbeau would say now if he knew what was going on . . .

Turnbeau didn't know what was going on, not at all. He sat in unit 12 of the Bideewee, muttering to himself and peevishly cracking his knuckles. He felt vaguely depressed, wondering if he hadn't allowed things to get out of hand, worried not only that Brashear had defied orders by leaving the room, but in the way he'd stormed out as well. He got up, the solitude and the need for alert vigilance getting on his nerves along with everything else, and traced with his eyes the same trail of blood which Brashear had earlier. He wanted Brashear back and hoped he would hurry, promising himself he wouldn't utter another damn word about cops or morality. Brashear had been right; he'd acted like a plastic saint sitting in the judgment seat, when he wasn't sure he half understood what was troubling the man. Brashear had to work it out himself. Yet he still couldn't shake the sense of something wrong, something badly wrong. Turnbeau rubbed his palms together, attempting to calm his suspicions, and then there was hard knocking on the door.

"Coming, Dan," he said. He unlocked the door unthinking, throwing it open with a big smile.

It wasn't Brashear standing there, it was a man with a hat pulled down so that the brim shadowed his face, and he was pointing a sawed-off shotgun directly at Turnbeau's belly. *Mary, Mother of God*, Turnbeau thought, he was as good as dead because he knew in that instant he had made a terrible mistake.

Then the man pulled the trigger and the muzzle exploded a slug of double-ought buckshot that blew a crater in his stomach, and Turnbeau screamed but didn't fly backward the way they do in the movies but folded up like a sack of feed the way it really happens, and he tried to scream again because the pain was so white-hot terrible, and the man turned and ran away.

Turnbeau lay against the open door, his head and shoulders on the cold concrete walk, and he didn't want to die like this. Inside the room at least, with a little grace and decency, but he couldn't seem to make himself move any longer, couldn't seem to do anything except sprawl uselessly and hold what was left of his intestines, not even conscious of the hot blood flowing from his nostrils and mouth and pooling down around the shreds of his flashy sports jacket, or the carpet on the other side of the jamb which was becoming a carmine lake. But Dan would be here in just a second, yes God, Dan would help him move, and he would tell Dan things, oh he had so many important things to tell him now when there was so little time. Please, Dan, please hurry, you must have heard that shot, it was so loud, and you must have heard it and you will hurry, I know you will Dan

Judas Cross

because I want to be moved and there is so much to tell you now that there's no more time left.

By the time Brashear had run up the driveway and rounded the corner of the wing, Turnbeau no longer cared if he were moved or not.

2-a

Brashear felt like the world's biggest shit.

He slumped dejectedly against the unmarked cruiser, palms pressed hard to the fender behind him as though bracing against Lieutenant Jules's anger. His ass had been royally chewed since the lieutenant's arrival, but it was minor compared to his own internal wretchedness—the loathsome, despairing certainty that he was as responsible for his partner's death as if he'd pulled the trigger himself. More than anything he wished he could do it over, could do it right and not leave Moss alone in the motel room. But he couldn't, no matter how desperately he might pray. Moss would have to stay dead, and he felt like the biggest shit in the world because of it.

He stared straight ahead, not hearing too clearly and not seeing too well, either, everything blurring together like landscape to a man with vertigo. He managed to make out the dark outlines of the two other squad cars and the ambulance which all had squeezed into the small parking area behind the motel. They were parked at angles, their head lamps high-beam accusations focused on unit 12, their flashers pulsing red off the walls and faces surrounding Turnbeau in the doorway. There was the police photographer undulating in a tribal dance around the corpse, blinking the strobe flash of his Polaroid and mumbling a chant beneath his breath as he paused for sixty seconds. There were the intern and the doctor, intern lounging on his chromium stretcher while the doctor smoked a vile cigar, both waiting their turns with bored expressions. There were the uniformed patrolmen from the squad cars, milling about like crashers at a cocktail party, almost outnumbering the bystanders, whom they kept ordering to stand back, go home, it's nothing, nothing at all, folks. And there were Nalisco and Schmidt frantically working among the bystanders, asking for witnesses, leads, facts, because a cop being murdered was something, was something very much.

Some of the crowd had left already, healthily sickened by what they saw. But most were staying on in their various states of undress, attaching themselves to the underbelly of violent death suckerfish style, and bleeding the chill and horror from it. They were lewd, Brashear thought dazedly as he watched. They were damned obscene, and God forgive me for having caused it to happen this way. *Moss* forgive me . . .

"—aware of my orders?" Lieutenant Jules was demanding harshly.

"Yes."

"Sir!"

"Yes, sir." His voice was flat, dull, painfully tight through the constriction in his throat.

"Stay in the motel out of sight, right? No telling what had happened to the girl, what kind of bum Quaker is, right?"

"Yes, sir."

"Well, now we know. He's a killer, Brashear, a cop killer. And you know who we've got to thank for that, don't you?"

Brashear nodded, gesturing with one hand in feeble excuse.

"Who gave you permission to leave your post?"

"Nobody, sir."

"You're not a rookie, Brashear. Why did you?"

"It was only for a minute, sir, to get some cof—"

"A minute!" Lieutenant Jules raged. "One lousy minute and Turnbeau gets blown in half! And the schmuck who did it gets clean away! And you don't know one damned thing! How, tell me how!"

"I don't know." It was almost a whisper.

"What kind of cop are you, anyway?"

Brashear knew that much. Moss had tabbed him perfectly

Judas Cross

just before he'd walked out in a foolish huff: half a cop. But he couldn't tell the lieutenant that. It was bad enough as it was, with Moss sprawled over there in his own guts, waxen limbs outstretched and fingers curled like dead spiders, petulant eyes closed tight against some last nightmarish thought. There was nothing he could say; there was no defense. He averted his head, wincing as he studied the barren misery of his soul.

"Damn you! You look at me when I'm talking to you!"

Brashear reluctantly faced Lieutenant Jules. He was a spare, spruce man in his mid-fifties, with a nose pinched at its bridge as if once he'd worn very thick glasses, and eyes disproportionately large and protruding as if those imaginary glasses were magnifying them. His hair was the color of dust, thin on the crown and growing out around the ears, indented in a thin line along the head from the pressure of an old-fashioned fedora.

At the moment, the lieutenant was kneading the wide brim of his fedora in his hands, holding it close to his chest in nervous deference to the fallen Moss. It was a sign of respect he paid whenever faced with disaster; the rest of the time he wore his hat with the obligation due a skullcap. It was pondered at the station whether he took it off to screw, but considering what his wife looked like, it was generally conceded he must. The looie was, after all, a man of strict habit. Besides the hat, he always wore the same kind of gray woolen suit winter and summer, and was studious in his appearance down to the monogrammed handkerchiefs rising rabbit-eared from his breast pocket. And then there was his ulcer. He must've been born with it and he would die with it, though certainly not from it. He fussed and fretted over it as he might a pet poodle, pampering it with half-gallons of milk from a portable refrigerator in his office, and it was pondered at the station whether he had a picture of it in his wallet, to be whipped out when friends would show snapshots of their children. The looie was, after all, a man of strict loyalty.

"Think, Brashear, think! A man, a car . . . You must've seen something!"

"No, sir. I looked around carefully when I left, but it was quiet. Quiet and still, so I didn't think that—"

"You bet your sweet ass you didn't think!" Then he asked, low and mean, "You sure it was just a minute you were gone?"

"Yes, sir. As I told you before, sir, I got as far as the front of the motel, to the sidewalk, when I heard the shot."

"Uh-huh. You're real sure?"

"Of course, I—"

"You sure you weren't someplace else for a half-hour or so? A bar, maybe, or with some girl you know?"

The whore's ten dollars burned in his pocket. "I'm sure."

"I won't buy it, Brashear! I won't buy that Quaker could conveniently return, kill Moss and escape, all in the time it takes to walk down to the sidewalk!"

"He didn't, sir."

"What?"

"He didn't just happen to come back. He was hiding around here all along, waiting to get back into the room."

"Brashear—"

"He'd have used a key otherwise. The room was dark, silent, like it was empty. He'd have used his key to get in."

"Maybe he thought his girl was just asleep."

"Then he'd have pounded on the door loudly, calling her name. Besides, the motel office is open; he'd have gone there first."

"Well, goddammit, who says he *didn't* use a key?"

"Moss!" Brashear gestured to the door. "Look at him!"

But Moss was gone, carted off in a black plastic body bag to the open maw of the ambulance. Brashear retracted his hand, wiping the back of it across his lips. "Moss would've heard the key or the shouting and stayed pat. But he was gunned in the doorway. He answered the door thinking it was me, probably, and never had time to draw. Quaker was ready for him. Quaker must've been aware we were in there, that there was one to buck after I left."

Froggish eyes narrowed, unblinking. "Why take such a risk?"

Judas Cross

"He must've been after something, something damned important."

Lieutenant Jules beat him to the rest of it. "It's got to still be in there, then. Dammit, we'll tear the place apart and find out. If we don't, we'll find out when we nail the bastard. But Brashear —I'll shove a billy club up your ass sideways if it turns out Quaker *was* hiding. What the hell did you do to make him suspicious? How was he tipped off there was anybody in there?"

Brashear considered Schmidt and Nalisco, the way they'd acted when relieved, then figured what good would it do to bring it up. "I can't tell, sir. We had the lights off, no television, just sitting in the dark and waiting."

"And dreaming of coffee and doughnuts!"

Nalisco approached, drawn and harried. With him was a plump, squat man whose oiled black hair accentuated flaccid, vanilla skin. He was clutching an unbuttoned raincoat to his breastbone with one hand; underneath he was wearing the pants of a suit and striped pajama tops, his feet in sockless shoes.

"We found a witness, Lieutenant," Nalisco said. "Only one so far, I'm afraid. Name's Hilton, Arlen Hilton."

"Like the hotel chain." The man's mouth, pink and full, quivered like the underlip of a cow.

"He lives over on the next street."

"Thirty eleven Claar." Hilton pointed a finger of his free hand at a house rising from the gloom behind the motel. The house seemed to have every light on, and the silhouette of a woman could be seen peering out of an upstairs window.

"We were looking for the way the killer went," Nalisco said. "Over there on the other side of the parking lot, you can just make out a little dirt path. It goes to his backyard, then along the side to Claar."

"Kids, you know. A shortcut; you know how kids are."

"Mmm," Lieutenant Jules said, not having kids of his own. "And you saw what happened, Mr. Hilton?"

"Not exactly. I heard the shot first. Terrible noise, not at all like a car backfiring or something like that. It scared me, in fact."

"Uh-huh."

"Well, I was just sitting there in the living room reading when I heard the shot. I rushed to the side window—it's a bay so I can see all around—and this man ran right past me on the path. He was holding a gun, a big one, like a rifle. I yelled at him to stop but he only raised his gun and shook it at me, you know, like he was threatening me?"

"Yes, sir. What did you do then?"

"Why, nothing. I told you, he had a gun. I'm no fool. I stayed where I was, watched him run across the street and get into a car. He drove away. That's it."

"That's it," Lieutenant Jules echoed, and Brashear saw his knuckles stand out as he clenched the fedora tighter. "What about the man, Mr. Hilton? Can you describe him for us?"

"Not much besides the gun. It was so dark out there, and he was running, you see. I only got a glimpse of him."

"Well, try. What was he wearing?"

"Casual clothes, as I recall. Some kind of thin jacket is all that comes to mind, like a poplin. Nothing fancy, just casual."

"Uh-huh. How tall was he?"

"Oh, taller than you. More like this fellow here." Hilton indicated Brashear with a nod. "Yes, big and tall."

"Six foot, then? Hundred and eighty pounds?"

"I guess."

"How old would you say? Thirty, forty?"

"I dunno. He wasn't a kid, though."

"I see. Did he have a hat?"

"No."

"Then his face— Did he have any scars? A mustache? Glasses?"

"Might have. I don't remember."

"What about his hair?"

"Average. Not too long like a hippy, but not too short either. He was . . . average, you know?" Hilton shook his head. "It happened so quickly . . ."

"Well, what can you tell us about his car?"

"I'm sorry. They look so much alike to me."

"Well, was it foreign or domestic?"

"Oh, American. I mean, there was nothing special about it, like it was a sports car or station wagon. Just a run-of-the-mill sedan; see one and you've seen them all."

"Color?"

"Dark, I think. He didn't switch on his headlights until he was out of sight, and there're no street lamps along there. I've been trying to get the city to install some, but they ignore me. Pay all those taxes, and they just ignore me. Maybe they won't after tonight."

"Maybe not, Mr. Hilton. Now, think carefully: is there anything else at all you can remember about him or his car?"

". . . No, I'm sorry. I was scared, you see, what with that shot and all, and then seeing his gun." He looked wanly at the lieutenant, then over his shoulder to unit 12. "He shot a man, didn't he? Kill him?"

Lieutenant Jules glanced savagely at Brashear. "Yes."

"Huh, how about that. Almost in my backyard. Why?"

"We don't know yet. Nalisco, you got this down?"

Nalisco licked the tip of his ballpoint and frowned at the note pad open in his hand. "It's all here, Lieutenant."

"Uh-huh. Well then, thank you very much, Mr. Hilton." He gave the rotund man a weary smile. "If you do think of anything more, please contact Detective Nalisco here. He'll give you his card."

"That's . . . it?" Hilton turned back, accepting Nalisco's card with reluctance. "I . . . imagine this happens to you fellows much? I mean, people not being able to remember lots of details?"

"Sometimes."

"I bet your laboratory scientists make up for it, though. Are they here yet? I don't see them."

"Our lab—? Oh, no, not yet. Do you want Detective Nalisco to see you home?"

"It . . . won't be necessary," Hilton said, seeming vaguely dissatisfied. He wandered off in the direction of the still-open door, side-stepping as the ambulance started and backed around. Its siren began from nothing, down at the very bottom of the scale, building gradually to a howling shriek; as the ambulance drove by the three detectives it sounded like the low, moaning wail of a long-ago steam engine passing in the night.

"Exactly how I feel," Lieutenant Jules muttered between his teeth. He took a deep breath, holding it as a shiver passed through him, then said, "Radio the description, Nalisco, what there is of it. Average man, maybe wearing a poplin jacket, Jesus H. Christ."

"Yes, sir."

"And while you're at it, get rid of Brashear."

Brashear had been staring at the retreating ambulance when he heard the lieutenant's words. There was a clammy taste in his mouth, had been all during the interview with Hilton, and watching Moss's final departure had only served to increase the emptiness, cold and bitter, in his heart. He swung back, eyes pleading.

"But, sir, I want to—"

"No! You're not staying. I don't want you here; I don't want you working on this case now or ever. It was Nalisco and Schmidt's to begin with, and they'll follow it up."

"Moss was my partner."

"He was Schmidt's a lot longer than he was yours." Lieutenant Jules glared, brutal and contemptuous. "Brashear, you want to keep your job?"

". . . Yes."

"You want to remain a detective?"

"Yes."

"Then get the hell out of my sight." He clamped on his fedora, fitting it precisely front and back with both hands, and stalked away, his face stolid.

Brashear trembled slightly, ashen-gray.

"Come on, Dan," Nalisco said gently.

"He was my partner."

"I know, I know." Nalisco opened the door. "Where to, home?"

Brashear's motions were numb, automatic, as he climbed into the squad car. He sat rigid, fingers caressing the knees of his pants. "To the station. My car's there," he said quietly when Nalisco started the engine. "I'll go home from there."

Judas Cross

"You will, won't you? No drinking or something foolish like that?"

Brashear didn't reply. They went around the corner of the building slowly, Nalisco eying him with care. "I . . . know how you feel, Dan. Moss was a little square at times, maybe, but a damned fine guy. Tough cop, too, especially in a pinch. We'll all miss him, that's for sure. Strange, him gone. I mean, I know it, but I don't believe it, if you know what I mean. But don't worry, Dan, me 'n' Abe'll collar this bastard Quaker if it's the last thing we—"

"Drop it. Just . . . drop it."

"Sure, sure."

They were almost at the motel entrance when Nalisco tried again. "Listen, Dan," he said. "I wanna thank you."

"What?"

Nalisco smiled tentatively. "Well, you know, for not telling the looie on me 'n' Abe. Hell, we were the ones who cooked up the deal with the manager, and one of us was always out for coffee or a smoke."

"Wouldn't have made any difference."

"Yeah, to the looie. So, thanks."

"It was my doing, not yours."

"I'm telling you, Dan, it might've happened to anybody. Just tough luck that Quaker chose you. A little earlier, and me or Abe could've—"

"Stop the car."

"But—"

"Stop the car!"

Brashear jerked the door open before Nalisco had fully braked, heavy nausea rolling in him. He staggered to the brick planter which ran along the side of the driveway, and stood sucking in air, staring sightlessly at the waist-high hedge of English bell heather. The heather had dark-red spears of blossom and ash-gray leaves. He puked all over it.

2-b

An opacus moon crossed Sanponset River with the crisp, chewing breeze, leaped above Steuben Hill and poured down among the inner suburbs, coasting along wide, tree-lined Frenchtown Avenue to wash the intersection with Wiletta Lane in a pale milky bath; then flowed along the smaller street's paved-over bricks and quarried-stone curbing to inspect the rising knolls of lawn and the tempered houses beyond. Some of the houses were built of wood, some of brick or weathered stone, but all were built in that cloddish, provincial style from between the wars.

The moon scrutinized the seventh house from the corner, clutching its front-porch columns and fingering the wire screen of its side patio and roving its rough backyard with streaks of light. A single beam filtered through the check-rail windows of the kitchen, spearing Brashear as he sat in the dimness of the Colonial breakfast nook.

Brashear gazed at the opaque pattern the moon painted on the alcove table and waited restlessly for his wife to get out of the bathroom. She had been in there when he got home, but the surprise of his early arrival hadn't seemed to quicken her any. What the hell do women *do* in the bathroom, anyway? Other than his nettling desire to see Valerie, Brashear felt drained and void. His initial oppression had passed with his sickness, leaving him not weary, not hopeless—just with the emptiness which comes from the realization there's nothing that can be done. All there was left was the moonlight, pearly and still as flesh, dead flesh seen in a motel doorway.

"Valerie . . . !"

"Not so loud, dear," came through the locked bathroom door. "You'll wake Lisa."

"Well, hurry up."

"I'm in the tub. I didn't know you'd be home now."

"I've been home fifteen minutes already."

"Don't be so impatient. It's not polite."

Judas Cross

It's not polite, for Christ's sake. Brashear looked up from the table and glared moodily at the locked door ahead of him in the hall and thought: That's Valerie all over. If it's not a locked bathroom door, it's a throat-held blanket or a swaddling negligee, or *something* to maintain the pretense of always being a lady. And a lady, according to that pucker-cunted mother of hers, was perfect and unblemished by sin or unlocked bathroom doors . . .

"Come *on*, Valerie!"

"I know, dear. I want to talk to you, too."

After six and a half years, Brashear knew what that meant. Give me, take me, buy me. No, better make it seven; she'd wanted to talk to him in that same tone of voice before they were married . . .

Valerie Gagnon had been a student assistant-registrar at Fairleigh Dickinson when they met, and Brashear . . . well, he'd been engaged to a hometown childhood sweetheart. He was standing in front of Valerie's desk that day, the overhead fluorescent highlighting her face and making her eyes a pale, glistening blue when she glanced up at him.

"My class changes," he said, handing them to her.

She tilted her head slightly as she read the paper, her face snub-nosed and puckish under a fall of wheat-straw hair. One hand rested on its back, fingers curved to hold a smoldering cigarette. Brashear felt a familiar beginning ache; and his fiancée was in upstate New York and he was down here, and what else is there for a bored, frustrated college senior except here and now?

She looked at him again questioningly. "Something else?"

"You're new, aren't you?"

"Yes. I transferred from N.Y.U."

Her skin was translucent, the pulse of her arteries pink like silken threads. He didn't know where to begin, his own blood beating in his groin. "I see you smoke," he said, and it sounded foolish to his ears.

She returned to scanning his class changes. "Mm-hmm."

"Do you drink?"

She answered without looking up, "Yes, a little."

"Then let's have dinner," he blurted. "Tonight. An Italian dinner with wine, since you drink a little."

She raised her head and pressed her tongue, just the tip of it, against her teeth. Then she leaned her body against the desk, folding her arms over her small, firm breasts as her tongue slipped softly upward against her lip. "Don't you want to know my name first?" she asked . . .

Thus had been his introduction to Valerie the girl.

It was less a passionate love than relief from loneliness and ennui which drew him to her, and he knew it would not be permanent. It could not; come Christmas vacation and he'd be back home with his fiancée. This was merely a holiday. Yet like most holidays, it was pleasurable to extend, even when he noticed a tension, an awareness building between them as the dates continued. Odd electric pauses developed, especially at mention of his fiancée, glances becoming more meaningful than words. It literally climaxed on Halloween night.

Three bottles of cheap champagne, of all things, were consumed at a small party beforehand, and three glasses alone were usually enough to make Valerie rather romantic. Later in his one-room, fold-down apartment they talked and finished some leftover Chianti . . . then came together in raw, spontaneous compulsion. He felt the heat of her breath against his cheek as he turned to brush her trembling, parted lips. She tried for a moment to twist away, but resistance ebbed as his hands rose to cup her tight, apple breasts, hardening their nipples beneath her brassiere. Her thighs ground involuntarily against his stiffening loins; with a faint moan of acquiescence, she wrapped her arms about his neck and pulled them both down on the couch, which doubled as his bed. It had seemed so natural at the time, so damnably inexorable for him to snake a hand around to the zipper of her dress . . .

Brashear had wanted their first time to be as sensitive and caressing as the press of her tongue against her lip. Instead the act of love proved savage and desperate, his a brutal force driving up inside her delicate body, a body which surprised him by its own urgent demands. And afterward Valerie had cried, but she told him she did not hate him or hold him entirely responsible. Had she been the stronger person she thought she was, it wouldn't have happened. She could have broken away if she'd really wanted to . . .

Thus had been his introduction to Valerie the woman.

Valerie came to him often after that, though never with wanton eagerness or abandonment. Always she was self-conscious of her need, and devoutly determined to subdue the crudity which had marked their initial violent coupling. They made love because of love, she said; and love was something too precious and fragile to soil. So she came to him wearing multilayered, floor-length peignoirs of innocent pastels; she came to him to be disrobed as gently as the softness in her downcast eyes; she came to him to be seduced by romance and deadened of her inherent shame. She came to him surrounded by candles and wine and music on WPAT, and Brashear discovered that he enjoyed it. He was occasionally gripped with an insane desire to rip off her clothes and throw her down and screw the toenails off her, cave-man style, but of the two, he preferred her way. It added a depth of meaning, a confirmation of shallow phrases by solid touch. The candles were the fat, incense kind that flickered with soothing fragrance in an otherwise darkened apartment. The wine was no longer dollar-a-gallon, but French and chilled in an ice bucket he'd been induced to buy somewhere along the way. The music was lush and infusive, like the sound track to a Hollywood bedroom farce of the late forties, and there were moments when Brashear felt he was living in one. He half expected to reach for her one time and find himself fading out . . .

Thus had been his introduction to Valerie the lady.

His fiancée grew increasingly unreal, only forcing herself accusingly on his conscience when letters arrived or had to be answered, and then assuming a remoteness of distance again. He didn't want to consider the dilemma rapidly shaping in the back of his mind, and he ignored it until just before Thanksgiving. Then Valerie wanted the first of her little talks with him.

"Dan, I want to talk to you. I missed my period."

It could be a case of nerves, of course. Yet she'd never

missed a period before, Valerie said, and her rhythm was punctual as the calendar. And in hindsight, precautions had admittedly been haphazard, contraception being too coldly logical for her romantic notions. But pregnant or no, Valerie had ended Brashear's holiday. He rode the bus home for Thanksgiving weekend a shattered young man, and incensed his fiancée with an unexplainable impotency.

When Valerie didn't begin bleeding the next week, Brashear took her to a doctor for one of those shots that supposedly starts overdue menstruations. When nothing happened, Valerie wanted another talk. Brashear slunk home for Christmas vacation and braved his fiancée for the ring back; Valerie sprung the impending marriage on her Calvinistic parents and learned that her pregnancy was the just punishment for her sins. Plans were hastily made. Valerie didn't upset them when her next period flowed right on schedule. She crossed her legs and kept it a secret.

Daniel Junius Brashear married Valerie Millicent Gagnon on January 12, in the United Baptist Church in Teaneck, New Jersey. Their first big fight occurred toward the end of the month. It was, understandably, over a box of Tampax.

As Moss had said: You can't be just a little pregnant.

So what does a guy do? He rants and raves and calls his new wife a lying bitch. He watches her face crumple and listens to her sobbing about love, she did it out of love and the fear she'd lose him to that other girl. He takes bitter consolation in the thought that most guys are suckered into marriage one way or another. He grudgingly admits she's pretty and a good cook and is for whatever he wants to do, including becoming a cop. He confesses, God help him, that he loves her, loves her very much. He puts his arms around her and pats her awkwardly on the back and tells her it's all right, darling, it's all right now. And when she finally lifts her head and looks up with puffed, pleading eyes, he gently leads her to the bed and bangs the crap out of her. That's what a guy does.

And by the time a year and a half later when Valerie had truthfully attained the shape of a Goodyear blimp, Brashear had experienced months of creeping guilt for having made such a stupid stink on their honeymoon. And when Lisa was born, he actually felt sorry that his wife hadn't been pregnant way back then. Lisa was a joy. His daughter would never be beautiful; as a baby she looked chunked out of metal, square, like an old-fashioned robot. But she was *his,* dammit; he'd created her, and she was beautiful to him, especially when he cuddled her softness to his cheeks.

It was he who pressed for more children. Maybe later, Valerie would tell him, maybe later when there weren't other, more important considerations. And she'd swallow the pill she'd learned to take so conscientiously. But the romantic games continued right along, no matter where they lived. The candles burned and the wine was chilled and the treacly music flowed through the bedroom. Brashear found himself a generally contented man—generally, because running counterpoint to the romance were the little talks.

"I want to talk to you, Dan. This apartment is too small . . ."

"I want to talk to you about a new dryer. We simply need . . ."

"The girls are meeting for bridge here next Thursday, dear. I want to talk to you about a sale I saw on . . ."

Three different apartments and then renting a house with an option to buy and then buying it; dryers and bassinets and furniture; slipcovers when the furniture didn't last, and then new furniture. It all takes money. So do doctors, repairmen, car dealers, and a vague persistence called "keeping up." There was always something for Valerie to talk about.

Two months into being a rookie and long before he became a father, Brashear was figuring the checkbook one night and suddenly yelled, "You're building a goddamn nest!"

"Don't swear at me," Valerie replied. "Besides, most of our friends can afford nice things. Why can't we?"

"Most of *my* friends are cops, and the only reason they manage is because most of them are on the take!"

"Take? You mean bribes? Graft?"

"Yeah . . ."

For the good of the system, a cop is taught about graft

immediately. First time out, Brashear was shown where food and stuff could be had, since the veteran who'd been assigned as his senior partner had to eat and smoke that day no different from the rest, and hell, the kid has to learn the ropes some time, don't he? The sergeant of his beat warned him right off the bat what crap games and cardrooms and cribs to lay off, because he didn't want some eager beaver screwing up a good deal for him and the other men on his rotation. Nothing worse than a square recruit with a bug up his ass.

At the time when Brashear was yelling at his wife over the finances, he hadn't made up his mind what to do about it. He didn't have a bug up his ass, but he was inwardly disturbed by the system and his own naïveté. It made him uncomfortable, uneasy somehow, the way Valerie felt about parading around naked.

Valerie wasn't uneasy about discussing it. "Do you take, Dan?"

"Not really. A pack of cigarettes or a free meal once in a while, but I got to get along with the guys. No money, though."

"You never told me this before."

"I didn't see any reason to," he hedged.

She looked at him with a curious expression, her tongue touching her lip. She walked slowly across and into the bedroom of their then new apartment, and Brashear heard her strike a match. For the candles, he thought. He heard her call out softly, "Come in here a minute, will you? I want to talk to you . . ."

God, the games people play.

Once in on the system, Brashear found the luxury of extra money turning into a necessity that was never quite enough. Now, after six-odd years of marriage, it still seemed that the more he brought home, the more Valerie could think of to talk about. Valerie had plumped out a bit with the birth of the kid, but he guessed that was to be expected, and she'd slaved on diets until she was within ten pounds of when they were married. She still had her clear ivory skin with tendril arteries, her exaggerative blue eyes, and the casual way of pressing her tongue against her upper lip when she smiled. Lisa had turned five this past August and was getting old enough to be fun as well as adorable. Brashear almost wondered if there was something wrong with him because he didn't feel any symptoms of a coming seven-year itch; he loved his wife and daughter, enjoyed the complacent security of home life and had no desire to see if some strange piece was a better lay than Valerie. He didn't know how much of it was due to the candles and wine and soft saccharine music, and he wasn't too interested in finding out. He intuitively feared that like a person, once dismembered it could not be reformed and live.

Like Moss had been dismembered and no longer lived . . .

The bathroom door unlatched and Valerie walked out barefoot, wrapped, like spring, in warm and tender saffron. The terry-cloth robe was tied with a belt of darker orange-yellow which was drawn around her waist, knotted, the short loose ends left dangling between her legs. She came from the mist of the bathroom with unconscious suppleness, averting her head and fussing with the back of her hair, her lips slightly parted in a languid smile the way women do after a relaxing bath.

She switched on the kitchen light automatically. "My, you're home early, dear. I'm so glad."

Brashear blinked in the sudden glare. "Come here."

He watched the belt as she walked closer, oddly disturbed by the way its ends swayed with the movement of her thighs. There was nothing overtly indecent about it; her robe covered her better than the fashionably short dresses she wore. But he felt a strange, momentary fascination in knowing she was naked underneath, knowing she had to be, and knowing he needed her so very badly right then.

"Why were you sitting in the dark?" She leaned over to kiss him perfunctorily on the cheek. "Aren't you feeling well?"

"No," he said, and reached impulsively for her. He tightened his fingers into the barely clothed flesh of her buttocks to pull her near, and sensed her reflexive stiffening, the stirring from his hands.

She retreated a few coy steps. "Now, Dan."

The demand for her crumbled in his grasp. "Valerie . . ."

"There's a proper time and a place."

"Valerie, Moss is dead."

That stopped her. "Moss? Moss Turnbeau?"

"He was shot tonight."

"Oh, no! Was it an accident?"

"Shotgunned point-blank in the stomach."

Valerie tightened as if something cold and clammy had rubbed against her spine. "How horrible. Were you with him?"

"Yes."

"And that's why you're home early?"

"Yes."

"You were with him when it happened. Thank God *you're* all right."

"Me? Me?" He turned viciously on his wife, unable to turn on himself more than he had already. "Look at me. You see lots of holes? You see me bleeding all over your nice clean floor?"

"Dan, you know that kind of talk makes me ill."

"Me, I'm fine, and thank you very much. It's Moss who isn't. Moss is in the morgue with his guts blown out."

Valerie was beginning to grow chalky. "Please, Dan. I—I don't care to hear about it."

"Don't *care?* You knew Moss, he was here plenty of times with his wife. Not the phony, ballbusting neighbors you prefer, but pretty decent people just the same. And you don't care?"

"Of course I care. I just don't like hearing about the . . . details, that's all." She clutched the throat of her robe, reminding Brashear fleetingly of fat Mr. Hilton. "It sounds so ugly the way you're talking."

Brashear looked down at his hands, empty, and squeezed them into fists. "Lieutenant Jules on my back, more worried about his precious regulations than a dead cop. And Nalisco pissing in his pants for fear I'd squealed. Jesus, it's like Moss never really existed."

"Dan! If you wake up Lisa with your swearing and she—"

"I wasn't with Moss actually, not the way I should have been. I was on the stakeout with him, but I took a moment off. Just a moment, Valerie, I swear it was just a moment off. But he must've been waiting for that moment. I told the lieutenant he must've been waiting all along, God knows why."

Judas Cross

"Who's *he*, Dan? The man who shot Moss?"

Brashear nodded, using his fists now to brace his head. He knew he wasn't making much sense to Valerie, that he was spewing it in a jumbled mess, but he didn't care right then how it sounded. It seemed more important just to chuck it out and be rid of it, like his vomit on the motel heather. "Yeah, the man. He killed poor Moss and I wasn't there to stop him. I was not there." And that brought him to the crux of his own personal agony. "I killed Moss, Valerie. Don't you see? I killed him."

Valerie was at a loss. She waited for him to speak again, but he lapsed into silence, dropping his hands between his legs and locking his fingers together. Finally she went to him, sitting down on the edge of the alcove bench and gently stroking the back of his neck.

"You did nothing of the sort," she said tenderly. "You didn't know what was going to happen, nobody could have. I'm sure you did what you thought was best at the time. You're a good cop, Dan."

"When I'm not on the take."

"I don't see what that has to do with it."

Brashear recalled the whore and knew. He rejected telling Valerie about her, though. Wives like Valerie equated whores with fruit stands, inherently suspecting that along with the money could come a pinching of the goods, a sampling of the wares. He had enough trouble without begging for more. "Nothing," he said. "Nothing at all."

"You know we need the money."

"Sure." His voice was thick and strained. "There's never enough. Not enough of it, not enough of me. Just as Moss."

"Dan, you're blaming yourself for nothing."

Brashear didn't answer, continuing his veiled, morbid meditation.

"It was a terrible thing that happened, but you mustn't go on like this, dear. You must forget it. Please, let's talk about something else now."

Brashear sank farther into the quicksand of his thoughts, letting Valerie caress his neck and ease the stricture of his muscles. He could watch her body beside him from under the corners of his lids; the dark belt of her robe flexed with the motion of her arm. Perversely, it began to affect him again.

"I wanted to talk to you anyway, about Lisa. You know she's in kindergarten, and all the other little girls have the most darling mother-daughter outfits from Spengler's this season."

This is hell, Brashear thought. Moss is dead and she's worried about what to wear to school.

"Dan, are you listening to me?"

"Shit on Spengler's."

"What a thing to say!"

"You I figured would understand. I figured my wife, a cop's wife, would at least understand and care a little. You don't."

"Stop this, Dan! I *do* care! Don't you care about your daughter?"

"Oh, God."

"Lisa's at a sensitive age. It's very important for her to be accepted by the other children."

Brashear wondered when a woman wasn't at a sensitive age.

"Daddy?" A thin, sleepy wail came from the depths of the hall.

"There, you proud of yourself now? You woke your child."

"*My* child. Christ." Brashear closed his eyes momentarily, leaning back against Valerie's stilled hand. He felt too exhausted to fight. "I need a drink. A big one."

"Go on, get drunk." She sounded nasal, like a whiny spaniel. "Why don't you see your daughter first? Why don't you explain to her why she can't look presentable at school?"

"Cut it out, Valerie." Brashear slid around and out the other side of the booth, and stood tucking in his shirttail while his wife inspected her nails with injured grievance.

"Daddy? Daddy?"

"Coming, princess."

"At least *I* think of her welfare . . ."

Brashear went from the kitchen without a backward glance. Coming home, he'd been afraid that he was going to have a tough time just facing himself, and now he was resentfully aware his wife wasn't planning to make it any easier. Still, it was his problem, his sweat; he had to try and put right what he could, keep Moss in the back of his mind somehow; he couldn't take it all at once . . .

At the end of the hall was Lisa's bedroom; she was sitting up in bed when he entered, looking to him like a fragile wraith in the white cocoon of her jammies. He sat down near the head of the bed and gently ruffled her dark-blond hair.

"And how's my little princess tonight?"

Lisa hugged him eagerly, his own dark eyes in miniature sparkling back like wet onyx stones. "Where's Zig-Zag, Daddy?"

Brashear chuckled. "In the hall closet."

"You're not going out again tonight?"

"Not tonight, princess."

"That's nice." She scrunched her urchin face against the sleeve of his shirt. "Did Mommy tell you?"

"About what?" As though he didn't know already.

"My new dresses. Two new dresses, and you know what? Mommy's going to get two new dresses just like them!"

"Well, we'll see."

"Tomorrow, Daddy?"

Brashear felt the remnants of his resolve melting away. "We'll just have to see. Now you go to sleep, y'hear?"

She reached up and kissed him on the side of his mouth, then snuggled under the covers. She watched him as he moved toward the door, just her eyes and nose poking out from between the sheets and pillow. "I'm going to dream about my nice new dresses," she said.

"You do that, princess, you do that." My God, it's all a plot. They really know how to zing you, and you don't have a prayer between the two of them, not a prayer.

The light in the kitchen was off again, but the door to their bedroom was ajar, and Brashear could hear Valerie softly counting to herself as she brushed her hair. A nightly ritual.

He pushed the door open, smiling wearily. "You must spend all day brainwashing that kid."

"Don't be silly, dear." She said it lightly, gracious with victory.

He unbuckled his pants and pulled his shirt over his head. "Listen, talk to me first before you talk to her, will you? I can't say no to both of you."

"I know." She was sitting on the scalloped-fringed stool before her vanity mirror, using a handled brush in long strokes like a girl keeping track of skip-rope jumps. Her robe had loosened a bit—on purpose?—and the mirror reflected the hollow of her breasts, which were snow below the tan line of sun.

Naked now, Brashear lay down on the wide double bed, stretching out past the open sheets to where the spread had been folded at the base. "You know, it's sort of chilly in here."

"Well, put something on."

"Why? I'm not going anywhere tonight."

Valerie put the brush aside and stood with easy grace, Brashear studying her as she moved about the room—the curve of her waist as she gathered up his clothing, the roll of her hips as she bent to light the candles on the bedside tables, the dusky outline of her back when she switched off the overhead light. The candles threw flames of sweet confusion against the shadows, and for the first time Brashear became aware that the clock-radio was on.

He rose on his elbows as she came toward him, determined to think of her and nothing more of Moss. But in the gentle intimacy of the bedroom, he found himself torn between listening to the muted sounds of music and the voice of feral death. His partner kept calling out of the darkness and then sinking back, only to call out to him again. Brashear forced himself to watch his wife, insisting on solely her, fighting madness in his mind.

"Darling . . . ?"

She was standing before him now, as close as she'd been to him in the kitchen. Again he was distracted by the desire to touch that darker stripe, gripped by the way it divided her body and parted her legs. He felt a hunger to open the robe and press against her, to smother himself in warm, breathing flesh and forget the other voice, the voice of cold, dismembered flesh, the flesh of his partner, his dead partner Moss.

The robe fell away from her body, pale and moist, and her lips were an inch away from his. She curled her arms around his neck, and he could feel the pulse of her breasts and the warmth of her palms against his face. I love you, she whispered above him. He became as a lost boy cradled in a woman's strength, hearing now her whispers, candlelight and music whispers, and pulled her down to lie alongside of him. She clung, one leg bent between his thighs and pressing against his tightened scrotum, and whispered again in ancient affirmation, I love you. He gripped his fingers hard upon her breasts and she pressured her legs and smiled with her tongue to be easy with her, easy. Easy, he aped in falsetto, and drew her needfully to him.

Her thighs rolled slowly outward, parting in gestured welcome. He could feel his erection being drawn up into her womb, driven by the force of her ankles locked around his calves and the tightening arch of her answering hips. I must forget Moss now, he urgently cried against her; I must think of only here and now and the times when I've possessed her like this, body quivering and thighs like budding flowers. She caught him between the gently squeezing muscles of her belly, urging him onward, upward into her moistened, ready cleft, and the thick scrolled candles licked burnished patterns on their naked coupling flesh . . .

. . . but oh the moment was short and then Jesus Christ it was rising out of him already. He could feel it boiling from his loins, and it was not the bursting of a thousand rockets or pounding waves against a beach or any of that nonsense, it was his semen, dammit, his semen already rupturing out of him and into her with all the fury and guilt and misery he had stored that evening. Moss, oh God, Moss. He shuddered against his wife with the anguish of his suffering, pressing harshly to her breasts, the milking sheath beneath him smooth and clasping, and then the peak declined, and with collapsing cries he was still.

"So soon?" It was an amused, lover's chiding.

He could not respond. He slid from her, his body lost of

hardness and shrinking into itself. And on the candles, the wicks of small flame devoured what remained of the soft, perfumed wax.

2-c

Life goes on.

A cop was dead, and in the squad room next evening, none of the other detectives looked especially vibrant either, but 'tis said that life goes on . . .

"He hurt me good," the girl complained, "and tha's a fact."

"I din' touch her hardly," the boy countered.

"Uh-huh," Robard said. He was back and looking as if he wished he'd stayed home sick another shift. He had a medium, off-the-rack build, though his clothes always seemed too small, and he had the kind of battered, square-jawed face that wasn't romantically craggy, just pugnacious and ugly. He casually brushed off his desk blotter, turning disinterested eyes from the girl on his right to the boy sitting on the other side of his desk.

"What's your name, son?"

"Esteban. Esteban Cabrera."

"What do your friends call you?"

"Where you got my frien's?"

"Downstairs for now. What do they call you?"

"Esteban." He was slim and wasp-faced, of Puerto Rican extraction, but sporting a black's processed hairdo.

"I want him arrested," the girl said. "I want him and his two punk pals thrown in jail, and tha's a fact."

"I din't do nothing. She started it."

The girl turned righteously livid. "*Who* started it? You did, you and your friends, pawing me like you owned me or something."

"Yeah, you loved it. 'Come over, why don'cha?'" he mimicked her. "'Come over while my ol' lady's working and have some fun, why don'cha?'"

"Well, I've got you down that you're disturbing the peace, Esteban," Robard said.

"Naw. Jus' a li'l party, *pequeño tumulto*. Nobody got hurt."

"I did, and tha's a fact."

Robard regarded the girl again. She was seventeen, of milk-chocolate complexion, mascara-eyed and haircut Afro. She wasn't often in the squad room, but most of the crew knew her: Glory Rhodes, a name her parents had inadvertently cursed her with at her christening. She was the revolving girl friend to an East Portlawn gang called the Blood Avengers, but wasn't above attracting outside action when bored with her soul mates. Which was usually the reason behind her visits to the precinct, and why Robard wasn't overly concerned this time around. He said, "Yeah, you sure do look real bad, Glory."

"Huh, that's all you know. I could show you if I had a mind to."

"Why don'cha?" the boy sneered. "Why don'cha show it to him likes you did for us? *Perra!*"

"You hear that? You hear what this monkey done call me?"

"Quiet!" Robard slammed his palm down on the desk. "Quiet, the both of you!"

Brashear glanced up from the report he was typing, momentarily startled by the noise. Schmidt and Nalisco ignored it. They were at their desks, preparing to leave on duty and carrying on some conversation they'd started at dinner; both being bachelors, they often ate dinner together at the restaurant across the street. And both being bachelors, it was a shame they weren't paying attention to the girl the way Carberry was. He was leaning against the water cooler, drinking from an empty cup and openly ogling her. Glory, silent for the moment, was tugging at the hem of her short skirt, wordlessly conveying what part of her had allegedly been damaged. As she squirmed her hips, her fleshy, braless breasts quivered in agreement, their black areolas and distended nipples puckering the front of her thin lilac sweater.

Brashear returned to the Supplementary Report DD5 that was one-third completed in his typewriter, determined to get it over with. Normally he would have been diverted by a pair of full breasts which jiggled as freely as Glory's, but Moss's death was having a more immediate effect, obligating him to finish this painful account of his debacle the previous night. The words refused to come. It was too depressing, having to relive it this way in print. Angrily he rifled through the carbons of other reports stacked in his IN basket, rationalizing that he was looking for an idea, a hook on which to start again, but knowing it was merely procrastination.

On top was Schmidt's Initial Report DD4, of the original complaint concerning Irene Jeliknek and the investigation of Turnbeau's murder. Then there were voluntary statements by the motel manageress and Mr. Hilton; a preliminary autopsy report filled with fancy words and no surprises; a lab report that the motel room was full of blood, flesh, and a thousand unidentifiable fingerprints; and a report from Firearms Identification. FI had matched the wadding and buckshot dug from Turnbeau's gut with a spent 12-gauge Remington Express shell found in the motel parking lot. Shell markings—firing pin, head space, ejector and extractor—indicated, though didn't prove, the make of weapon; FI's guess was a Marlin Repeating, perhaps the model 120. But by the relative wide pattern of shot and the close proximity of the ejected shell, they did determine that the shotgun had been sawn.

Then there was the interview with Irene Jeliknek, transcribed at the hospital that afternoon. Love. She'd attempted suicide out of love and a dread that her Johnny wasn't returning. No solid reason to suppose that; he'd told her he'd be away on business for two weeks, and she should know, she was his secretary, wasn't she? But no word from him, no card, no letter, no phone call, nothing. It had built up in her, ten days alone in the motel room, waiting, not knowing, feeling sordid for having lived in sin, and fearing he'd dropped her for the slut she was. She was sorry now. She was sorry she'd caused so much trouble, sorry she'd wasted her emotions on a man like him. No man was worth it, she saw that now, and now it was bitterness that bled from her veins.

Below that was a photostat of Baltimore's Telex, answering

Judas Cross

the request for identity and background checks. Irene Jeliknek: no local arrests, no complaints, clean. Recent graduate of Hathaway Business School, first position at J. Quaker Co., Baltimore, and described by her roommate as reserved and religious and a bit of a prude. And John Quaker: no local arrests, but not so clean. Address given on motel registration confirmed as being both home and office; as a self-employed manufacturer's representative, he worked out of his own house. Divorced twice, known to his neighbors as an extrovert and a drinker, preferring loud women and louder parties when he was around, which wasn't often.

It fit. Brashear could readily imagine Quaker sizing up his new young secretary with covetous eyes, challenged by her prim innocence after all the easy lays he'd bagged, seeing in her a latent hot streak which just hadn't been turned on before. That she'd eventually succumb wouldn't have been the question, only how soon and where, and he'd have flattened her to a bed like a well-oiled steam roller. It fit. It fit just dandy.

The hell it did.

There was the FBI package under the Telex, showing that Quaker had taken a fall twenty years before in Ohio, for felony, burglary. Sentence suspended, as he'd been a minor then with no previous trouble. And none since. That was a rub, because usually there's a pattern to these things—a man works up to blowing holes in cops. And then there was the fact that the motel room had been swept to its studs, right down to the medicine-cabinet slot where you slide your used razor blades, and nothing important or incriminating had been discovered. Which, as things currently stood, left one brass-plated sonofabitch and one motive for a silly girl to try suicide over him. Yet absolutely no motive for the brass-plated sonofabitch to return, wait in ambush and blow holes in a cop. So it didn't all fit, and that was very depressing, too.

But just in case, there was a round-the-clock guard posted with riot guns at the motel. Just in case that bastard had the balls to show up again . . .

"That's better," Robard was saying, calmed. "Got a job, Esteban?"

"Oh, yeah. I work at the car wash, on Pollard. We all do."

"So you were driving around after work and picked her up, is that it?"

"Nobody have a car. We was walking." Esteban curled his lip slightly. "If we'd have a car, we'd been nowhere near this *mamapinga*."

Schmidt, who'd finally noticed Glory's breasts, laughed at the boy's obscenity and inadvertently farted into the cushion of his chair. Nalisco, behind him, wrinkled his nose. "Thought at dinner you liked the meatloaf, Abe."

"I did."

"Better a second time, though."

"I need more'n the eggs you had."

"You can't ruin eggs, Abe, not even the cook over there can."

"Eggs get monotonous."

"So do you two," Robard said, swiveling around. "Hello, Mr. Gallagher; hello, Mr. Shean. Your act smells worse than the meatloaf."

It smells, all right; everything smells, Brashear thought sourly as he listened to their sniping. It smells of the sweat of pressure, pressure exerted by themselves as much as from higher up. It smells of the gaminess of growing frustrations and impatience, and the acridity of fraying tempers. It would be fresh air and sweetness once Quaker was nabbed because of course Quaker was the source of the smell. He had to be, because if he wasn't, there was nowhere else to look and then there'd *really* be a stink. So Quaker was it, or so they'd been convincing themselves for the past twenty hours. But it was strange how a pungency of something wrong nested in the air; of something fitting wrong, of something smelling wrong.

The door opened and a man entered the squad room. He was dressed entirely in gray—dark-gray suit, pale-gray shirt with a pearl-gray tie, even his hair was iron-gray. He walked to the slatted railing, smooth and baby-faced and smiling a salesman's glad-hand smile. But the hands gripped the railing nervously.

Nalisco said, "Something we can do for you?"

Judas Cross

"Is this where murders are handled?"

"Yes, sir."

"The murder last night?"

"You know something about it?" His voice was suddenly tight.

"No, not really, but . . ."

"But what?"

"I heard that you're looking for me. I'm John Quaker."

A silence, a pallbearer's silence, shrouded the room. And with it came another smell, the burned electrical smell after lightning has struck.

"Well?" Quaker asked.

"Jesus," Nalisco said, and went for the gate.

Schmidt rose long enough to take back the stack of reports from Brashear's desk; they were his, Brashear being unauthorized to have a set since he wasn't on the case. Carberry threw the paper cup away and dragged a chair over to Schmidt, and Brashear contemplated moving closer, too. But he stayed where he was, Turnbeau's empty desk an insurmountable stone wall between him and the action. The squeak of Moss's chair leaning back, the curses over the wobbly goose-neck lamp . . . Odd, but the invisible things were the mortar between the stones, holding him back.

Robard was busy throwing the two youths out as fast as he could, tired of their meaningless squabble, anyway. Esteban was grinning; Glory was not. "I've done been had," she said indignantly, "and tha's a fact!"

"You've been had plenty," Nalisco added as she strutted through the gate. He held it for Quaker, then snapped it behind them and ushered him to a chair next to Carberry. "I'm Detective Nalisco," he said, drawing his chair to hem Quaker between them. "And this is Detective Schmidt. We're the ones handling the case."

"Yes," Quaker said, seeming very unsure about the whole thing.

Schmidt glanced through the reports with nonchalance, as if unimpressed with Quaker's presence. Nobody else said anything. Maybe Quaker didn't know it, but Brashear and the others were well aware he shouldn't have come in like this. A guy will bury the hatchet in his wife or such, then feel compelled to confess from overwhelming grief and guilt, sometimes before the corpse is found. But not with this deal. It fit less than all the other things which didn't fit, so it was quiet for a while—a deceptive, nasty kind of quiet as everybody stewed and the smell became worse.

Quaker shifted his eyes from Nalisco to Schmidt to Carberry and back again, finally averting them downward and plucking nonexistent lint from his suit lapels. When he wasn't looking, Schmidt said, "Nice of you to come in, John."

"Well, why shouldn't I?"

"You tell us."

"Tell you what?" Quaker's eyes were rounder now, uneasiness growing in them. "What is this?"

"Tell us where you've been, John."

"Traveling. That's my business, traveling. I handle a few lines of import radios and appliances, things like that for the electronic stores." He took a business card out of his breast pocket and laid it in front of Schmidt. "I come up this way every quarter or so, take in Philadelphia and Camden, swing through Burlington and Gloucester counties, then up the Jersey shore."

Schmidt flipped the card aside. "What about last night?"

"Well, I was in Ventnor. I must've canvassed a half-dozen stores there yesterday."

"Fine," Nalisco said with an edge, "but what about last night?"

"Ventnor! I had dinner at the Prime Rib, I always do when I'm there."

"With a customer?"

"No, with . . . a friend."

"What's your friend's name?"

"Myrna, but look, I don't want her—"

"Myrna what?"

"Myrna Cusick."

"You had dinner with her, and then what'd you do?"

"Afterwards? Well, we had a few drinks here and there, and then went back to her place."

Judas Cross

"For how long?"
Quaker licked his lips. "All night."
"All night, huh?"
"Yeah, you know how those things are. I heard over her radio this morning about it up here, and left soon's I could. Jesus, it was some shock."
"I just bet it was," Nalisco said. He tilted back and picked up the Sanponset *Evening Record*, and began to roll it into a tube. "So what's this Myrna's address?"
"Look, I don't want you bothering her."
"You can prove where you were another way?"
"No—no, I guess I can't. But take it easy; if her husband ever finds out . . ." He made a slicing motion across his throat.
"Shit, one down here and a married one in Ventnor. He's got them stashed all over," Carberry said, and plucked the rolled-up newspaper out of Nalisco's hand. "Where's her husband, Quaker?"
"Out of town. He's a trucker for one of the freight yards in Atlantic City."
"Shit," Carberry repeated, and lashed Quaker across the face with the paper. Quaker's head snapped to one side and he lost his balance, nearly falling out of the chair. Carberry caught the man by the jaw with his left hand, tilting his chin up and compressing his cheeks. "You're a sweetheart, you are," he said and let go.
Quaker's hands went to his reddened face, his eyes blurring with water. "What was that for?"
"I was married once"—and left the rest of the reason unsaid.
"What's her address, John?"
"But you can't—"
"Damn right I can!" Carberry cut in. "I've a badge that lets me split your head open for assaulting an officer. Here, right here in front of four witnesses. You understand?"
Quaker rubbed his cheeks, glaring and sullen. "I want a lawyer."
"You've right to counsel after you're in custody," Nalisco said. "You're not in custody now."

"Yet," Schmidt said. "What's her address?"

"It . . . it's on Cedar. I don't know the number, but it's in the phone book."

"Sure, the Yellow Pages. Seen your girl yet?"

"My girl?"

"The one you dumped at the motel, sweetheart."

"Oh, *her!* Irene's not my girl, she's my secretary."

"Not for long, she isn't. Seen her?"

"Irene? No, not yet. I told you, I drove right here."

"She cut her wrists, you know."

"I can't understand it."

"Yeah."

"I told her I was coming back. We were going up to New England for the rest of my swing, but hell, I've been turned on to Myrna for years, long before Irene. I mean, I didn't see any reason to end a fine thing just because I was with her. How was I to know she'd fly off the deep end?"

"Is that what she did, over you?"

"It must be. I mean, I was . . . her first one."

"You shit," Carberry said, and with elaborate slowness sliced Quaker across the face, then backhanded him with the paper again. Quaker yelled and covered his face; Carberry rammed the butt end in his stomach, doubling him over, making him rock in the chair. "I oughta wire your balls to a light socket and see how you turn on, sweetheart. Killer."

"I . . . I didn't kill your cop, if that's what you're thinking."

"Somebody did."

"I—I don't know who."

"It looks different to us, Quaker."

"It looks wrong."

"Why'd you do it? Why?"

"I didn't!"

It was Nalisco who hit him this time, a rabbit punch that sent Quaker sprawling to the floor. "You had a full day cooking up an alibi with some two-bit whore who gives head-jobs, but it won't work, not with us. Thirty seconds, and she'll be spilling her guts to get out of an accessory rap."

"No—no, it's the truth . . ."

Judas Cross

"You must've had a reason to kill him. Come on, Quaker, tell us what really happened."

"I . . . I have, I have." Quaker was gagging, sucking in air.

"Why'd you come back to the motel?"

"Where's the shotgun, Quaker?"

"I didn't . . . I didn't . . ."

"You did!" Carberry raised the paper again. "You did!"

Brashear moved. He didn't know why he was out from behind his desk and moving, the act spontaneous and compulsive. Perhaps it had something to do with seeing Quaker curled helpless on the floor, and a vision of Moss similarly displayed at the motel. Or the quick remembrance of loose bricks in a dirty motto. There was no time to consider; the act was done and he was grasping Carberry's wrist, jerking the arm up and away from Quaker.

"Lay off, Ed! It's not the way."

Carberry twisted around, light dancing in his eyes. "Let go of me," he said, strangely smiling.

"Stop it, Ed." Brashear felt the ache of clenching teeth. "If Quaker has an alibi, let Abe check it out. Working him over isn't going to change anything. It's not the way."

"Tell me, Dan. Go on, tell me all about how to be a cop."

"Cut it out!" Robard pounded his desk again, this time with a fist. "I won't have it, not as long as I'm catching. You, Dan, let go. And you, Ed, back off. Dan's right, it's not even your case."

Carberry stared at Brashear for another moment, his face tense in a rigor-mortis grin. Then he relaxed, dropping his hands and flipping the newspaper onto Schmidt's desk. "Yeah, yeah," he sighed, sitting down. "I got a little carried away, I guess."

Nalisco gripped Quaker by the shoulder padding. "Up, you."

Quaker rose slowly, very pale. "You can't frame me," he said, slumping in his chair. "You can't arrest me for anything."

"Think again, John," Schmidt said. "There's Myrna."

"What? Since when was that against the law?"

"For years and years, John. It's called adultery."

"Come on, I'm not even married."

"No, but she is, according to you. If either party is married, it's worth one-to-three and/or a thousand-dollar fine."

67

"You guys would hang a saint."

"Only sweethearts," Carberry said in a low voice.

"Then there's this." Schmidt opened a bottom drawer and lovingly placed the Ruger Magnum on the blotter. "This yours, John?"

"Never saw it before in my life."

"We found it in unit Twelve."

"Don't know how it got there."

"Irene does. She told us how it got in with your socks."

"All right. *All right!*"

"Why'd you have it?"

"Protection. I carry lots of samples with me."

"Uh-huh. Why was it with her this time?"

"She . . . was a little scared, being by herself. I thought it might make her feel better, having it around."

Schmidt caressed the blue-steel finish. "No need to ask if you've got a permit, John. It's against the law for a felon to possess a gun, any gun for any reason."

Quaker jerked upright. "Felon?"

"Cincinnati," Nalisco said, "twenty years ago."

"That was nothing! Just a prank, me and a bunch of kids!"

"You were convicted of a felony, John. There's no statute of limitations on the Weapons Control Act of 1923."

"But it's always good for a year, sweetheart."

"God, God."

Schmidt stared at him expressionlessly for another moment, then turned away. "Somebody get rid of this *putz*."

"I'll take him downstairs," Nalisco said in a tired voice. "Hand me the Ruger."

"Indian giver." Schmidt slid the gun across almost reluctantly.

"Can't win them all, Abe," Nalisco said, and then took Quaker by the forearm. "Come on, lover, stand up."

"What? What? Where am I going?"

"To call that lawyer of yours."

Quaker nodded, wordless. Brashear watched Nalisco lead him out the door, a man grown smaller and walking with an air of having been overwhelmed, as if stepping from a craps table, wiped out.

Schmidt sighed, tilting back and closing his eyes. "Well?"

"Well what?"

"Well, he's not our boy."

"Sure he is," Carberry said, and then to Robard, "What do you think?"

Robard, who was dialing the lieutenant at his home, glanced up from the phone and said, "I think we better get busy checking him out."

"He'll be cooling his heels here awhile."

"Don't count on it, Ed. He'll be out on five buck's bail."

"Hell. Ain't right, letting a killer free like that."

"Some killer."

"Don't tell me you swallow his song and dance, Abe. We've had a pickup out on him and his car for over a day now—you think he could drive all the way up the Garden State Parkway in broad daylight without being tagged?"

Schmidt didn't reply; his pointed look was answer enough.

Brashear returned to his desk and lit one of the Chesterfields he'd bought in the Alley Cat. He'd said nothing so far, and had nothing to contribute now, finding no desire to thrash it out and pool his ignorance with the others. He couldn't help it; it was as though he weren't a part of it, or perhaps that he was but on a different level than they. He drew on the cigarette with nervous inhalations, retiring in his chair like a spider to a dark corner of its web.

"He denies everything, sir," Robard was saying into the phone. "Yes, sir, we're keeping him on ice on a couple of small ones. We'll tear into his alibi with everything we've got." He paused, listening, then: "Abe, pass me the newspaper, will you?"

Schmidt tossed the rumpled paper onto the other desk. "You know, if we can't crack his story, we're right back where we started."

"Back further, with nothing."

"Maybe it was revenge, somebody Moss arrested once."

"Nobody knew he was at the motel. It *has* to be Quaker."

"Sir, I saw the headlines . . . Yes, sir, we're aware what the commissioner said . . . What? . . . Yes, sir, he's here . . . They're all here . . . I know, I—" And then Robard hung up harder than he had to.

"What's his beef?"

Robard glared at Carberry. "He wants to know when the party's over."

"How's that?"

"He wants to know what the hell you're all doing here!"

"Well, Jesus, just because he's got alum up his—"

"Can it! Abe, either you or Nalisco's going to Ventnor."

"Not me."

"All right, not you. Get on the horn and set it up with them, somebody's doing some traveling tonight. Then we'll start combing BCI and our files. The looie's right; if Quaker checks out clean, then we've missed something somewhere. You can take the Convictions file, pull any that Moss had to do with."

"Gee, thanks."

"I'll dig through the Resident Criminal file," Brashear said, "see what comes up."

"The hell you are. I will, because I have to stay around here, but you're going out like always. No horsepuckey about dropping everything because it was Moss who got it, you know what the looie had to say about that. We relax on the rest, and they'll run all over us in no time."

Brashear opened his mouth.

"I know, Moss was your partner and you're itching to get a crack at it. That's another reason the looie wants you off the case. No vendettas, things like that, not with Wilcox and his committee farting blue flames at us every chance they get." He didn't add that Lieutenant Jules still had Brashear engraved on his shitlist, or that the lieutenant had called Brashear an incompetent asshole over the phone. He was being kind; he knew it, Brashear knew it, and so did the others, and it made him feel uncomfortable. Gruffly: "Now, you and Ed move out before he calls back."

"Me and Ed?" Brashear said.

Judas Cross

"There an echo in here? You and Ed. You're partners now, according to the looie. I'm supposed to break in a new man Metro's sending over tomorrow. What stoolies did Moss use?"

Brashear appeared not to hear.

"Dan, am I boring you?"

Brashear said lamely, "No. There's Snatch."

"Snatch?"

"Victor Sanchez, we call him Snatch. Then there's Racehorse Browne."

"Don't tell me he's still around."

"Yeah, slower than ever."

"Well, find them, see if they know anything. And keep your ears open in the bars just in case this is a grudge thing. You might be able to pick up something."

Carberry, reaching for his jacket, said, "Yeah, preferably blonde and stacked."

"Will you get your mind off your pecker, Ed?"

"Better go easy, or you'll give *me* a grudge."

"God Almighty, isn't one comedy team enough? Get out of here, will you, and look alive!"

Walking down the stairs a few minutes later, Carberry grunted and made a gesture with his thumb in the direction of the squad room and Robard. "He thinks he's King Shit tonight."

"Heat's on," Brashear said, "and he's catching."

"He sure must've from the looie." Carberry grinned, adding, "Where're your boots and black leather?"

Brashear, beard combed and wearing a sports coat and slacks, did a little Chevalier soft shoe on the steps. "Zig-Zag, 'e is under zee weath-air tonight. Meet Pierre Grenouille from Paree."

"Pierre, eh? What size shirt you got, Pee-air?"

"Forty-three." Brashear responded immediately with the European equivalent of American size seventeen.

"Not bad, not bad." Then Carberry laughed, the previous enmity toward Brashear seemingly gone. "We'll knock them dead, partner; tonight we'll knock them dead . . ."

Brashear tried to, but couldn't help himself as he walked out of the station house with Carberry. He glanced behind him on the steps, up at the stone façade. The motto seemed on the brink of collapse. Shivering, he sucked in the cool night air, but its freshness failed to dispel the odor that clung tenaciously to his nostrils.

2-d

Myrna Cusick had never heard of John Quaker.

Myrna Cusick was of Polish extraction, primely overdeveloped the way some Mid-European girls can be, and thickening now that she was past twenty-one and married. That wasn't quite how Nalisco described her afterward, when he was back in the squad room; then he referred to her as a "fruity little bitch." But at the time she was standing in her living room before Nalisco and the Ventnor police, she defiantly swore to God she had never heard of John Quaker. She was a good wife who would never dream of cheating on her husband, much less spend the night with a strange man. Oh, no, she'd been home alone the whole evening, watching television.

Right. So Nalisco, the Ventnor police and God, listed the cocktail lounges they'd already checked, and showed the credit card receipts Quaker had produced, and asked if she'd mind letting a few bartenders and waitresses have a look at her—the few who recalled a man of Quaker's description in company with a buxom young lady in a skimpy green dress. To which Myrna stoutly refused, insisting that a woman of her character and reputation could never be sullied by such outrageous degradation. To which her husband, back from his truck run and listening to all of this, punched her in the face.

Right. So the truth emerged along with a mouse around her eye. John Quaker's time was fully accounted for, and whatever else he was, he was not the killer.

The odor surrounding Moss's death became decidedly riper.

"The hell of it is," Schmidt said as he peered out the Cadillac's side window, "that we don't know what we're looking for."

Judas Cross

"Nothing from the stoolies?" Nalisco asked.

"Nothing," Brashear said. "Nothing at all." He was gazing out the other side window, Nalisco and Carberry wedged between him and Schmidt on the wide back seat of the limousine. Lieutenant Jules and Robard were up front with the chauffeur, stolidly staring through the windshield. They were the fourth car in the procession, preceded by Mrs. Turnbeau, her minister, and an assortment of relatives, and followed by friends, more policemen, and a reporter or two. It was one of those too bright, blustery days of autumn which remind you of springtime, with clouds thin, whitish veils unable to blur the sun but giving the sky a diffused and milky look. Brashear thought abstractedly that it was all wrong. It should be somber and gray and perhaps raining, the way it always is in the movies, but not like this. Somehow, it gave the funeral almost a sense of futility.

"Well, we can hope." Nalisco made a spasmodic attempt to cross his legs, but he was hemmed in too tightly and was forced to settle for tapping his teeth with a thumbnail. "Either from the stoolies or from the files, we've gotta hope we find something."

"Still checking the files?"

"All the way back, Ed," Schmidt said, "and Moss sure put away his share. Most are in the jug or scattered around the states, but too damn many are still floating around here."

"I still think it has to do with this Quaker deal."

"Maybe, but I don't see how."

"Well, I don't see how the killer could've been after Moss."

"Maybe he wasn't. Maybe it was a nut. You know, after the first cop he found."

"Not even a nut. You think anybody respects us any more? Not between the Wilcox Committee and the riots in East Portlawn last year, they don't. Give a man a ticket and he hates you."

"Anybody might've done it, anybody at all."

"Don't say that. Jesus, just don't say a thing like that."

Brashear could hear tires echoing across gravel as they passed the stone cairn entrance to Brook Park Cemetery. The harp-shaped gates were weathered and dulled, but once an ironsmith had pridefully ornamented them with fancy scrolls, giving them the appearance now of a drab old woman with a Byzantine necklace. Inside, the land rolled like a twisted rug, peppered with chalky marble crosses and ashen wood markers that were planted so thickly that the feet of one corpse must have been resting on the shoulders of another. The few deciduous trees here and there had been stripped of their foliage by the wind, leaving their stark, barren fingers with the appearance of blight. They were, considering the day and Brashear's own despondent mood, vaguely comforting to him.

The Cadillacs parked in a semicircle, not far from a hollow where a few people were gathering around a mound of earth and a shallow pit. The six detectives looked down to the grave site for a moment, and then started for the hearse.

"We didn't have to be here," Lieutenant Jules said, low and savage. "We didn't have to be running around in circles, trying to find out if it was Quaker or a grudge or a nut, and worrying if somebody here will be next. And I trust that somebody here realizes it."

Brashear chilled from the accusation and the conviction it was deserved. Occasionally these past three days, he'd found the death impossible to accept, Moss being gone too stunning to be true. But more frequently, he'd been overwhelmed with a personal sense of responsibility, and a frustration at being ordered from the case. He felt the need to help set things straight, as if he could somehow make it up to Moss, and Moss could somehow absolve him at least a little bit that way. Such a time was now, hearing the lieutenant and fumbling for a silver handle on the oaken casket. He trudged behind Nalisco, down the gentle slope, one of six solemn men with whom Moss had worked, one of six who carried the weight of his coffin between them. But the one who alone carried the greater weight of profound inner guilt.

Brashear stood across the open grave from Mrs. Turnbeau, the wind fitful and elusive, eddying around his dark-blue suit, toying with the legs of his pants. Florence Turnbeau was a thin, breastless woman bleached with heartache, dressed in black almost to the ankles, her head held rigidly as though it might fall. Her face was tired, hurt, lined with that expression of

Judas Cross

having cried herself dry but still wanting to cry some more. Her eyes were perceptively puffed around the lids, tiny lines threading from the outer corners and reaching for her temples. The thick pancake make-up covering her grief was smeared, rubbed too often by the handkerchief knotted in hands clasped in front of her.

She was flanked by a minister and the one relative Brashear recognized, a brother from Detroit he'd once met. The brother's face was corrugated and brown from overexposure to the weather; the face of the minister looked exposed to nothing harsher than hot towels. The wind sucked ancient laments from the minister's mouth, scattering myth and memory inaudibly over the rows of indifferent dead. They lowered her husband on canvas belts, and she stared silently down at the box, which held him to its cold satin bosom, until the symbolic trowel of earth spilled across the lid. Then she turned away, hazel eyes blinking painfully in the sunlight, and everybody filed after her up the hill while gravediggers shoveled in nonsymbolic dirt to cut off Mossam Turnbeau from a lovely autumn day, the kind of day when you were glad to be alive.

The mourners gathered before dispersing to pay last respects to the widow. She shook hands with them wearily, glancing into each face with a curious expectancy, as if hoping one might miraculously become her husband. Brashear fell in line with reluctance, staying toward the back with the hopelessness of not knowing what to say. What do you say to a friend's wife after the friend has died, after the *way* your friend has died? Something meaningless, he supposed; a quickly blurted apology of pitiful inadequacy, and then move on.

His turn eventually came, and she lifted her eyes to face him. "I knew it would end like this, without reason." Her voice was fragile with the threat of collapse, and he could see the film of water as she tried to stall her welling tears. "I just knew it would someday. Men, there's trouble in all of you."

"He was as good as they come, Flo."

"I should know, twenty-three years of being wife and mother both to him. I'm forty-two years old, forty-two, and for the last twenty-three . . ." The tears were pooling in her eyes now, causing her to blink rapidly. "There's trouble in you all. And let me tell you something. I think he was stealing, I think he was stealing on the job."

"Flo, you're not making sense. You're mistaken."

"You'd say that, you'd stick up for him. Just like a man," she said, and the tears riveleted down her cheeks. "F-forgive me, I know I'm not making any sense. I can't be sure, I can't be sure of anything any more. When I'd ask, he always handed me some half-baked excuse. Coming home after working on my feet all day, there were too many other things to do than to spy on him."

"Not Moss, Flo. Believe me, not *ever* Moss."

"Maybe so. I can't be sure. How can I? Food to cook, clothes to wash and iron and sew . . . Best I could do just to drag myself into bed every night after he left."

"I understand."

"Do you?"

"I do."

"I wonder if you do. All I ever wanted out of this life was a little happiness and contentment, but it seems I'll never get any. I'm forty-two and I'm tired, old and tired, and there was no reason for him to die. No reason at all."

"I'm sorry."

"A little late for that now, isn't it?"

"Flo, please. What can I say?"

She began to sob earnestly now, choking, the tears squeezing between tightly shut eyes to flow down her face. "Sorry. Of course you're sorry. I'd be sorry too if I were you. Does it bring Moss back to me? Does it?"

The knife twisted in his gut, and Brashear felt helpless and exposed, a shriveled eunuch. "I . . . I'm *sorry*, Flo." He turned, nervous and seeking escape.

"Don't you *dare* walk away, Dan Brashear!"

"I'll come by later in the week, Flo, with Valerie. It'll be better then."

"No, I want to talk *now*, all the trouble you've caused!"

"Please . . ." He looked around despairingly. "Reverend . . . ?"

Judas Cross

The minister wrapped an arm about her as if to hold her up, but she didn't look in danger of falling. There was an ashen rigidity to her like stoneware, her eyes glassy and almost vicious. "Yes, yes, Mrs. Turnbeau. Is there anything we can do?"

"Give me a reason! Give me one, just one! Do you know one?" And then she crumbled against the minister, hands kneading her handkerchief, weeping into his frock as the tears coursed freely down her contorted features.

2-e

Night arrived, crying.

The rain Brashear had morosely half wished for the funeral began inexplicably during the evening rush hour, not hard but steady, causing a spurt of rear-enders and fender-benders. It was still falling a few hours later, a fat drizzle bursting on the unmarked police cruiser like cat's-paw prints, giving the uncomfortable impression of driving beneath a soggy gray sponge that was continually being squeezed. The siren was on, drowning out idle conversation and most of the garble from the two-way radio. Brashear leaned against the armrest, silent, his thoughts preoccupied with that afternoon. Carberry drove with swearing regard for the newly slickened pavement, past a series of taverns, auto garages, and clapboard houses with signs for their first-floor stores hanging like stained laundry from their second-story windows. Battery Street was polished and glittering under the glare of the headlights, but the overcast had smoothed the scabrous buildings on either side.

Carberry parked across the street from 877 Battery, Pelican Jewelers, an ambulance and squad car having lined the curb in front of the store. Their red lights were flashing, reminding Brashear of Moss's death at the motel with an empty, queasy feeling in his stomach. They hurried across to the store, which was a skinny structure set flush to the cracked sidewalk and leaning slightly to the left, against a used-appliance shop called Joel's Trading Post. The lights were on and the door was open, a patrolman shielding himself from the rain by standing guard on the threshold. A plastic tag over his left breast named him as Akin, G., but they already knew him from the station.

"Ten-ninety," Akin said, meaning it was a burglary. "Owner arrived unexpectedly while it was in progress, and they clouted him a good one. Think it'll let up any?"

"Not for a while. Where's your partner—inside?"

"Murtagh's up the street someplace, checking to see if anybody saw or heard anything. I hear it's really coming down up by Pompton."

"Uh-huh." Brashear paused to scrape an obstinate gum wrapper off his shoe sole. He glanced in the windows, which were empty save for a poster card of a pelican. It had a tiny cotton ball glued to the top of its beak, and a motto beneath the webbed feet reading: "A little down on a big bill." The rain rolling down the glass in front of it was like tears, dripping from the chin of the sill. It made Brashear think of Florence Turnbeau, and the way she'd cried.

"Ambulance attendant is inside, though," the patrolman continued. "Taking care of Lederman. Jesse Lederman, he's the owner. In that little office back there, behind the counter."

"Thanks." They stepped into the shop. It was mostly a series of glass cabinets formed in a U-shape and boxing in the front door. Around the walls were colored religious pictures and novelty clocks. A little down on a big bill, easy payments, easier repossession, and the pussycat clocks rolled their eyes and wagged their tails, come on, come on. The glass of the cabinets wasn't broken, but the backs were open and velveteen trays were scattered over the linoleum floor, barren.

The office was a small partitioned square hiding a desk, chair, adding machine and safe. The safe was an old Mosler, its boxcar wheels on short planks of wood, its staggered door wide open. An elderly man sat in the chair, hands flat on the desk for support and showing their hairless, liver-spotted backs. His white shirt was unbuttoned at the collar, unraveled bow tie almost as red as the bloodstains on the cloth. Bent forward to allow the attendant to tape the back of his head, the aged tendons of his neck showed like corded steel in the light.

Judas Cross

"Okay if we talk to Mr. Lederman?" Carberry asked the attendant.

"Sure, it's okay," Lederman replied instead. He made the slight clicking noise of dentures too old or too cheap or both. "I imagine you want to hear what happened, don't you?"

"Yes, sir."

"Cleaned me out, that's what. Came back here after dinner and there they were, cleaning me out. Don't normally come back, but I got a special shipment of watches in today, and I wanted to finish checking them in before I opened tomorrow. So I came in the alley door, saw one out behind the counter and yelled at him. I didn't see the one hiding behind the door. He's the one who hit me."

"Did they have guns?"

"The one behind the door did. That's what he hit me with."

"What kind was it? Revolver or automatic?"

"It was big, black, and hurt like blazes, that's all I know."

"I think that should do it," the attendant said, closing his black cabinet bag. "You should see a doctor, though."

"Why? What's wrong with me?"

"I don't think anything is, but we recommend it."

"Sure." Lederman watched the attendant leave, then said, "Nice boy, did a real nice job bandaging me, or I'd show you where I was hit. Whanged me a good'n, let me tell you."

"Yes, sir. Can you tell us what the men looked like?"

"Boys. They weren't more'n boys, twenty-five or the likes. One was tall and the other was fat. Meaty fat, you know what I mean? Both were white, wore them blue bib overalls, the kind that fit over your regular clothes."

"Did they wear glasses or have beards?"

"Nope, no glasses, and they were clean-shaven. Wore cloth caps pulled down low, like Jimmy Cagney always had in them gangster films he made. Pretty smart, wearing them overalls. Just dump them later, and nobody'd know what you had on underneath."

Carberry looked up from his note pad. "They say anything to you?"

"The tall one never said a word, but the fat one, he said, 'Get in the office and don't cause no trouble.' Then he said, 'Open your safe or I'll hit you again.' I did. No reason to've hit me the first time, I'd have done what they told me."

"Did he have an accent?"

"Nope, talked like everybody else. Had a tattoo, though. Saw that low down on his left arm, near the wrist. Tattoo of a dagger through a heart, plain as day. You think he might be a sailor?"

"Too soon to tell, Mr. Lederman. Is there anything else you can recall about either of them?"

"Nope. Just a couple of young smart alecks."

"What did they take?"

"I told you, they cleaned me out. Eighty, ninety dollars from the safe, but that doesn't bother me as much as the stock. They emptied the trays into big canvas sacks, and I had a nice selection of diamond wedding sets for the coming holiday season, my good time of year. And all my watches, too, even the new batch."

"You have the case and movement numbers of the watches?"

"Yes, but they're mixed up by brand name right now. I can have a list for you tomorrow."

"You want to call this in, Dan?" Carberry asked.

"Fat chance. I called last time, it's your turn to get wet."

Carberry grumbled routinely as he walked away.

"What time did you leave here, Mr. Lederman?" Brashear asked.

"Five-thirty, same as always. I came back at seven-forty. I know that on account my missus likes that new situation comedy show. Me, I can't stand it, so I left and it takes me ten minutes to drive here."

"Did you see anybody loitering around?"

"Not when I left. There was a car parked in the alley next to Joel's when I came back, though."

"Theirs?"

"I suppose. I heard it roar off soon's they'd left. But I'm afraid I hadn't paid it any attention. I didn't know anything was wrong at the time."

Judas Cross

"You locked up before you went home?"

"Tight as a drum. And set the alarm, not that it did any good. It never went off."

"What kind do you have?"

"Strips of electrical foil on the windows, gadgets on the doors, a big bell out front in a cage. Cost me plenty, too."

"Why didn't it go off, Mr. Lederman, do you know?"

"Oh, sure." Lederman rose ponderously, wincing as if suffering from an acute hangover. He walked unsteadily out of the office and through another doorway, where he switched on a bare overhead bulb. Brashear saw they were in a narrow storage alcove that butted against the office partition. A rear door was open and another door along the side was slightly ajar; both were of thick oak with heavy locks. The side door connected with the Trading Post. Its wood was gouged and splintered around the handle and locks, and the jamb was cracked almost in half.

"That's where I came in," Lederman said, pointing to the rear door. "But they bust through Joel's place, pretty as you please. I guess I was foolish at the time, but I didn't have an alarm gizmo installed on the connecting door. Thought I'd save a little money, figuring Joel'd be smart enough to wire his place, too. And what the blazes, that's solid hardwood with two separate locks on it. Didn't seem to stop them though, did it?"

Brashear walked through the appliance store, past rows of abused washers and refrigerators and the musty odor of stale grease and packing. The Trading Post's alley door had been jimmied, and there was no sign of any type of alarm system. He peered out into the now deserted alleyway. The rain sounded hollow as it drummed down between the buildings and puddled on the uneven pavement.

Brashear returned to Mr. Lederman, shaking his head. "We'd like you to look at some pictures at the station, see if you can identify them."

"If it'll help catch the smart alecks. Must be something wrong with them to hit an old man like me, wouldn't be surprised if it was the way they're raised, that it was all their parents' faults."

"Maybe. We'll settle for them."

Carberry came in, wet, especially about the shoulders and the saddle of his back. He shook his hat, spraying water over the floor. "Got out the broadcast, called the lab. They're on their way now. Murtagh is bringing in a woman."

The woman was in her late forties, with a heavy jaw, pronounced nose and dull brown hair which hung in frizzy ringlets. Her paisley-print housedress covered a beefy figure shapelessly, its only decoration a silver medallion pinned between gelatinous breasts.

"This is Mrs. Fish," Murtagh said.

"Alvina Fish." Her voice was a tart contralto, her tone brooking no argument. "My husband is not ap-preciating this, believe you me."

"We just want to know what you saw, then you can go back home."

"A car, that's what I saw. It came shooting out of the alley while I was crossing the street. I looked both ways like you're told to do, but it came shooting out at me without no warning a-tall. Almost knocked me down, and I dropped my groceries, I was so scared. Went chasing after it, too, yelling for it to stop. Not that it did any good."

"Could you tell what kind of car it was?"

"A year-old Chevrolet Impala, one of them fancy ones."

"You're certain, Mrs. Fish?"

"I should be. Marvin, he's my husband, Marvin's been driving one since we bought it new. Not the fancy hardtop, but the plain four-door se-dan, but I know the car, believe you me."

"What about the license?"

"It had one."

"Do you happen to remember any of the number?"

"Now, what do I look like? It's raining, the groceries are spread over kingdom come, I'm running after it, and you expect me to memorize a thing like that? I ain't no gen-yus, you know."

"No, ma'am."

"You'd love for me to have it, wouldn't you? You'd dearly love it."

"It would be a help, yes."

Judas Cross

"Then it was a good thing I was so sore I wrote it down, isn't it?" Alvina Fish smugly produced a sodden scrap of grocery bag. On it in large, uneven pencil was a license-plate number.

It took Motor Vehicles two minutes to furnish the name and address of the licensee.

"Stupid," Carberry said, once they were back in the cruiser. The siren was off now, allowing him to be heard. "Stupid as they come."

"All three of them."

"Three? I thought there were only two, Dan."

"I'm including Lederman and his chintzy alarm system."

"Oh, yeah. It serves him right, the cheap bastard. I wouldn't doubt they never knew about it, either, just lucked out."

"Luck, my ass. They'd have done better if the bell had rung and scared them off. They've managed to jack themselves up to Burglary One with assault, probably armed robbery as well."

"Don't forget reckless driving."

"Hit-and-run, if you count the groceries."

Carberry laughed. "What d'you bet Grosvenor's one of them?"

Virgil Grosvenor was the licensee of the Impala that matched the plate number and description Mrs. Fish had supplied. R&I had radioed that he'd been picked up once on suspicion and twice for misdemeanors, gambling and drunk driving. Of course his Chevy might have been sold during the last few days, too recent to have been recorded, or it might have been stolen and simply not reported yet. It might have . . . but Brashear had the same feeling about it that Carberry did. This was strictly amateur night.

"No takers, Ed."

"Hell, I'll even bet the car's in Grosvenor's driveway when we get there, and him and his pal are in the house scarfing up beer. A pair of real jerks. I ask you, where's all the mystery and excitement I see on the TV shows about cops? Not on this job, not catching a pair of punks like these two."

Carberry kept on grinning, obviously in an expansive mood. Brashear couldn't believe his partner had ever considered police work more adventurous than it was. He could remember his own naïve youthful notions of action and romance and the dedication to battling Evil Forces, but not so Carberry, not even as a boy. Without the dreams there cannot come the disillusionment, and in no way did Carberry strike him as being discontent with reality. He was too rooted in it, too settled and secure with it.

Brashear watched him from the corner of his eye, aware that he was staring more intently than he should. Carberry didn't notice; his attention was focused on the dank night beyond the windshield, a cynical grin of easy battle drawing his lips back over his teeth, his teeth clenching the tip of his cigar with blunt obstinacy. This was the kind of investigation on which he thrived—no puzzle, just simple and direct, about as subtle as an elephant's prick. After two nights with Carberry as his partner, Brashear thought that might be an apt description of Carberry as well. It had been vastly different working with Moss, and the comparison reminded Brashear of Moss's comment concerning Carberry, that he was half a cop without the other half to know any better. It was an odd comment, and it bothered him.

Carberry interrupted his thoughts, oblivious to them. "We're at Clearwater, Dan," he said, turning the wheel. "Keep your eyes peeled for number Seventy-eight."

Brashear checked the houses with his brooding eyes. Clearwater was a short dead-end street in a tract development designed to be obsolete ten years after it was built, and that had been fifteen years ago. Seventy-eight Clearwater was similar to 76 and 80 and all the others: a dusty brown box with a dirty brown lawn of bald spots and untamed weeds. Some sort of deflowered vine fought with the unpruned shoots of cow vetch for the latticework of the sagging porch. The only other thing on the porch was a girl's bicycle, the rear wheel of which was nearly flat.

"You lose," Brashear said.

"What?"

"You bet the car would be here. It's not, so you lose."

"Huh," Carberry said, and wrenched open the front gate.

Roots of an oak tree had cracked the walk and lifted rough

edges. They stepped carefully, mindful of its being slippery as well as broken, then up the three steps to the porch. The doorbell didn't work. Brashear knocked on the frosted glass, holding the fly screen open with his foot. The lights were on and there was a muffled noise of occupancy, but no answer. Carberry flicked the butt of his cigar at the tree and Brashear knocked again, harder.

"Sis! Somebody at the door!"

There was a clatter like a dish falling, a pause, and then: "Well, clean it up, Fumbles." There was another pause before the door opened and a woman in her very early twenties stood wiping her hands on an apron. "What do you want?"

"Are you Mrs. Grosvenor? Mrs. Virgil Grosvenor?"

"If I am?"

"Is your husband home?"

"No, and I don't know where he is and I don't care. Why?"

"I'm Detective Brashear and this is Detective Carberry." He showed his identification. "We'd like to talk to you."

She pursed her lips in momentary wariness, then said in cold resignation, "I guess I can't stop you. Come in and sit down, I'll be right back." She left them at the door, walking rapidly toward the kitchen while muttering under her breath.

Brashear closed the door after Carberry. The living room had cheap, credit-house furniture that was cluttered with magazines and junk. The heat was on too high, making the air stifling and clogged. On top of a television console was a framed wedding picture; Carberry casually picked it up and then set it down again without comment. From where he stood, Brashear thought the portrait looked stiff and impersonal, as if the passage of hard times had sucked the individuality from the couple.

Mrs. Grosvenor reappeared without her apron. She was wearing a pair of tight pink slacks and a low-cut pullover which bunched at the sleeves and beneath her breasts. Her legs were bare, her shoes those black slipper-flats that curl up like sow bugs when removed. In the way clothes can indicate the meaning of a woman to a man, Brashear was struck by a vision of how she must look without them on. She had a certain gritty earthiness about her; the vision of her naked was not repellent.

"So what is it?"

"Do you own a Chevrolet Impala, license KAR313?"

"Oh, it's that. A repo. You cops moonlighting off duty?"

"No, ma'am. We're not here to take back the car. We want to locate it and your husband."

"I told you, I don't know where he is, and if he has any brains, he'll keep it that way. Imagine the nerve of him, wanting me to wash an undershirt reeking with some woman's cheap perfume."

"Is that right." Carberry said it lightly, eyes studying her.

"If I never see him again, it'll be too soon."

"Where does your husband work?" Brashear asked.

"Don't make me laugh. If he could get paid for parking on his butt, he'd be rich."

"Where does he park it?"

"Not around here. Sometimes I've caught up with him at Jack's Trap, over on Fourteenth. Neighborhood bar, not bad." She seemed to notice Carberry's brassy gaze, and returned it. "Who knows? You might find you like it once you try it."

"Yeah, I just might at that."

The flippant exchange was exasperating to Brashear. Curtly he asked, "You know anybody whose arm has a tattoo of a dagger?"

"That sounds like James. Wally James."

"Is he a friend?"

"Virgil's, not mine. You find one, you've found the other."

Carberry gestured toward the portrait. "We'd like a picture of your husband, to know what he looks like."

"Like the bum he is." She crossed to pick up the portrait, then turned with it in her hands and leaned against the cabinet. The arch of her body thrust her breasts outward, the press of her legs outlining her almost boyish thighs. Brashear sensed it had been a conscious move; Carberry licked his lips. "You can have this one," she said, and gave the portrait to Carberry.

Carberry handed the portrait to Brashear, his grin of before becoming leaner and somehow more wolfish. "We'll return it."

"Do me a favor and lose it. Look, not that I care, but he's not done something wrong, has he?"

"Has he?"

"Virgil? He ever did, you wouldn't have to come after him. You'd catch him in the act." She placed her hands on her hips, rolling them slightly. "My kid sister's here tonight, or I'd offer you guys a drink."

"Thanks anyway, Mrs. Grosvenor," Brashear said.

" 'Most any other night, and I'd be home alone."

"Too bad," Carberry said. "Guess a girl like you gets lonely."

"Especially a girl like me who likes company."

"Kid sisters aren't everything. Yeah, it's a shame."

Virgil Grosvenor smiled out at Brashear, tall and lanky in his tails, with kewpie-doll lips and a nose like a linoleum knife. Brashear glanced back up at his partner and Virgil's wife with increased irritation, sensing what was brewing between them and disliking it. It made him feel awkward and stupid, standing there uneasily like a cumbersome and unwanted chaperon. It also made him feel unclean, as if he were using bathwater after somebody else.

"We'll be going now, Mrs. Grosvenor," he said, as much for Carberry's benefit as for hers. He brought out one of the cards printed with his name and station phone. "If your husband returns, will you call us at this number?"

"Don't hold your breath."

"Nice to've met you," Carberry said at the door.

"When you're in the neighborhood, drop around for that drink." She was looking directly at Carberry. "I mean it. Any time."

"Yeah," Carberry said. "Yeah."

Going back to the cruiser, Carberry laughed out loud, then said, "You're not sore, are you?"

"No."

"About me beating out your time?"

"No."

"It's every man for himself, something choice like her."

"Sure."

"Jesus, you are sore, Dan. I can tell."

"Forget it." Brashear opened the passenger side and looked at the portrait in his hand again, at the too young couple with their fingers linked possessively together. He tossed it on the seat before getting in and slamming the door.

"I wonder about you," Carberry said as he backed the cruiser around. "Sometimes I really do."

Brashear slouched, arms folded, and wondered about himself, too. What was once a vague discomfort from the precinct motto had been welling since Moss's death into an acute resentment toward he knew not what. It confused him, becoming muddier and yet deeper as he realized he was reacting to more than just his partner's lust to lay a suspect's wife. He could feel its presence if not its content, like a preying tumor on his mind. Give me a reason for death, Florence Turnbeau had cried at the funeral; Brashear found himself echoing: Give me a reason for life. The problem of what one lives for gnawed at him with a sense of tension, even though he angrily told himself it was futile, a morbid waste of time . . .

Fourteenth was the market row for the development, at its south end and near the falls. There were bars about every other block, their neons staining the glossy walks in front of them, no more different in their own way than the houses in the tract. The locals would go to their choice with their wives or girls for a slow beer or idle gossip, or if hungry, for boiled eggs and leathery sandwiches. When they'd located Jack's Trap, Carberry circled the block, and on the return side street, they found the Impala.

"Stupid," Carberry repeated, shining his flashlight through the windows. "You'd think they'd have the brains to hide it."

"Probably don't even know it's hot." The interior was empty, and when Brashear tried the doors, they were locked. "The stuff must be in the trunk. Shall we get them to open it?"

"Yeah." Carberry laughed. "Want a beer, Dan? Come on, I'll buy you one. I know a joint that's just around the corner." They walked up to 14th, their shoes making slapping sounds on the wet pavement. "What'd I tell you, Dan. Some fat adventure with

Judas Cross

these clucks, too dumb to ditch their own car after a heist, eh? Pounding leather, that's all it is. Speaking of that, you should've worn galoshes tonight, like me. Help save your shoes, Dan."

"No thanks. Can't stand the things."

"Well, they're your feet. Don't blame me if you catch cold."

Brashear thought: That's Carberry for you, crime and galoshes in the same breath, of equal importance. Moss had been right about him, and yet wrong at the same time. The part Carberry lacked was due not to ignorance, but to indifference. He simply didn't care. This indifference did allow an enviable amount of dispassion while working, a certain unfettered objectivity. And hadn't objectivity been the core of his own argument with Moss? Yes . . . but then it would follow that indifference made Carberry the better cop. The meat of that logic stuck in Brashear's throat, even as much as he wanted to swallow it. He wanted to convince himself that indifference was the only practical attitude toward his job, the only effective compromise toward living in this world of grays and shades. For him to deny it would lead him in Moss's direction, begging questions he couldn't bear to ask, much less find the answers for. It was a fundamental chaos too swift and dark to risk examination . . .

Jack's Trap had originally been the front half of an old Victorian house, and as a consequence it was made up of three interconnecting rooms rather than the usual single long one. Its only other claim to personality was a décor of hanging horse collars. Brashear and Carberry studied the main section—the men slouched forward at the bar to view the television better; the couples in the booths surrounded by smoke and conversation; the trio at the shuffleboard table; the loner hanging on to the jukebox. None came close to resembling Grosvenor or his fat buddy. The bartender stopped mixing drinks and came over to them, his face polished and pink and suspicious because they weren't regulars.

"What'll it be, gents?"

"Virgil and Wally here?" Carberry asked.

The bartender hesitated, as if debating whether to admit he knew who Virgil and Wally were. "Cops?"

"Come on, are they here or aren't they?"

"Sure don't look it. You look like everybody else." He paused again, tilting his head. "Why do you want them?"

Brashear, already provoked, snapped, "If we wanted you to know, we'd have told you. Now, where are they?"

"Oh. Yeah. They're here. Fourth booth in the room to your left."

"Alone?"

"Last time I looked they were."

"What're they doing?"

"Drinking. Got some food with them, too."

"Thanks for the cooperation."

The bartender made a baleful expression. "Any time."

The room on the left was smaller and without a bar, containing five booths against the inside wall and a bowling game against the other. Grosvenor and James were where the bartender had said, having a grand old time over tap beer and hero sandwiches. They were out of their overalls, but their cloth caps hung on hooks on the outside of the booth support.

"No question, it's them," Brashear said. "Sitting ducks."

"Acting like it's a big joke," and then, as though unable to believe it, Carberry said again, "Stupid as they come, by God."

They approached the booth, coats unbuttoned. "Grosvenor?" Brashear asked the thin one with the sweet lips and hooknose. "You Virgil Grosvenor?"

"Who wants to know?" the fat one interjected.

Carberry said to him, "You give the first answer, we'll give the rest."

"Yeah," the thin one said, "I'm Grosvenor. So what?"

"You're under arrest."

Both men erupted out of the booth, no longer laughing, fear glinting in their eyes. James came like a tackle, thick shoulders hunched, and Brashear went inside a wild swing that was sent like a pitcher's overhand throw, bringing his own arm up to block it while punching with his right, but James slipped on the beer which had spilled, so that Brashear got a taste of nothing but air. Off balance, he bumped against Carberry, who had Grosvenor in an arm lock and bent over the table, and James rushed with a "Liverpool kiss," head to the belly, backing

Judas Cross

Brashear to the bowling machine as Grosvenor wormed loose and tried for the exit. "Shit!" Carberry said and grabbed Grosvenor again, turning him around and driving him back against the booth. James fumbled for the gun which was half out of his pants pocket, and Brashear kicked him in the stomach while aiming for the balls, doubling James over as the gun slithered across the slick floor. Brashear straightened the fat man by his shirt front and hit him twice more in the solar plexus before letting him fall. James went down and lay gasping fishlike in the beer. By the time Brashear had retrieved the gun, an old .38 Colt revolver, Carberry had stopped strangling Grosvenor.

"I must be getting old," Carberry said, panting faintly.

Brashear thrust James beside his buddy. "I know what you mean."

"You? You're not any older than they are."

"Thanks." Then to the men: "Turn around, hands flat on the table, and step back two paces." They frisked them down, finding no more weapons other than a small jackknife. "Now empty your pockets and count the money out of your wallets."

Grosvenor and James, surly and reluctant, piled their belongings on the table: keys, change, wallets, cigarettes and matches, and $187 in mostly small bills. Brashear picked up Grosvenor's key ring. "These to your Impala, Virgil?"

"I own a Ford."

"Sure you do," Carberry said. "Quite a lot of money there for punks like you. Where'd you hit besides the jewelry store?"

"It's ours, fuzz, all of it clean."

Carberry rapped James smartly on the ear. "Show respect, Wally."

"Straight on," Grosvenor said. "We can account for it. We got it together so we could leave this hole."

"Going to leave your wife broke, huh?" Brashear said.

"Screw her."

Carberry grinned, expecting to do just that. "Put your junk away, then hands behind your back."

Cuffs snapped on their wrists, they were hustled through the ring of gaping onlookers and out into the rain. "Lucky,"

James said. "You're just lucky. Once we'd eaten and split, you'd never have got us."

"How'd you find us, anyway?"

"Like your friend says, Virgil. Luck."

The cruiser was parked four cars behind Grosvenor's Chevrolet. Carberry held the back door open for the prisoners, taunting Brashear: "I'll radio for a tow truck, and a squad car to take them in. You can go check the Impala, it's your turn, remember?"

"You're sweet," Brashear said, turning up his collar. "Cancel the bulletin on the Chevy while you're at it, and the stakeout on Grosvenor's house."

"Yes, Daddy."

Brashear walked up the street and opened the trunk. Two large canvas sacks, tied at the necks, were nestled inside like Christmas in reverse. It was too sopping wet to take the time to open up the obvious; he could hear ticking from the self-winding watches that had wound themselves by the motion of the car. He doubted very much that all of the cash in Grosvenor's and James's wallets was their own, but that was another matter, and he pushed the deck lid shut and started back to the Dodge. He could see the hazy outline of Carberry now, sitting at an angle to the two men in the rear. They were doing something, he could not clearly determine what, and yet, oddly, he had the sick feeling he didn't have to, that he already knew. He quickened, hoping he was wrong and afraid that he wasn't, irrationally asking himself why Carberry would stoop to such a thing, why his partner would compound what was already bad enough with Grosvenor's wife and make it worse.

And when he met the thick, heavy silence inside the car, and saw an arrogant, derisive shine in Carberry's eyes, he had the sinking sensation that he was right about it. And when the tow truck was grappling with the Impala, and the prisoners were being herded to the squad car, he overheard Grosvenor petulantly whisper to Carberry, "Don't forget us, you promised."

"Sure, sure."

James's bleak expression belied his tone. "You give us the shaft, cop, and we won't forget you. And that's a promise."

"Shut up," Carberry said, and pushed them inside the squad car. And watching them being carted away, Brashear no longer had the slightest doubt about it, he was absolutely certain. Back in the Dodge again, and before Carberry could pull away from the curb, he said in a cold, dull voice, "You did it, didn't you?"

"What?"

"Christ's sake, Ed, I'm not blind. How much did you take them for?"

"Oh, that. Hell, I was going to tell you later, over coffee," he said, more defensive than necessary. "You didn't think I'd hold out on you, did you? I'm no welsher, I always split with my partner, you know that. Didn't I last night when we busted up that sex-swap party?"

"Yeah."

"And with Jaimie's policy bank the night before?"

"How much, Ed?"

"I just don't want you getting the wrong idea, Dan." Carberry kept the car at idle, taking out a roll of bills and counting them with his thumb. "Hundred and fifty. Here's your seventy-five."

"I don't want it."

"Now what's crabbing you?"

"You don't have any intention of helping them, do you?"

"Are you kidding? I can't, there's too much against them."

"But you took their money."

"Sure, I took their money. What's wrong with that? They're crooks, aren't they? What's wrong with taking money off crooks?"

"Some of it is Lederman's, for one thing."

"Well, you just go ahead and try picking out the bills that are his. Besides, you remember him telling us the money isn't so important; his insurance will cover it, and he'll be too pleased getting his junk back to worry. Go on, Dan, take your cut."

Brashear studied the treacherously extended dollars—tempted, yet averted by the guilt and confusion which had been plaguing him against his will. "No, I don't want any of it, Ed."

"What is it with you? You're acting awfully innocent all of a sudden, Dan. You know as well as I do, you've got to grab what you can when the chance comes along. Is it that you're afraid they'll bitch? Let them; by the time those suckers catch on, it'll only sound like window dressing."

Brashear turned his head away. It was more terrible than ever inside him, and there was no decent answer he could give to either himself or Carberry.

"Is it that it's more than we usually get at one clip, is that what's eating you? Well, what the hell, so what? It's no different than being on the cuff any other time."

Brashear stared out the windshield, the street ahead seemingly shrunken under a shallow curtain of rain. There *was* a difference, he wanted to retort; there *had* to be. He wasn't certain exactly how, other than what he took helped grease the wheels, while Carberry's careless yet calculated attitude toward graft did not. It was unjustifiable, and if Carberry couldn't see that basic difference, then he was not merely uncaring, he was as ignorant as Moss had said, no more aware of the nature of his compromise than the blind are of yellow. He had his goals—to lay Mrs. Grosvenor and buy a new car every three years—but goals are not ethics, are not values. He was, half without knowing it, complacent in his empty cell, so ignorant and blind that he considered himself and the cell one and the same, and more tragically, whole and complete. He could spot the need for fresh underwear, but not the truthful concept of himself. If he, Brashear, were no longer what he'd always supposed himself to be, at least he was able to realize it. And Moss had told him that as well, hadn't he?

"Yeah, you were all the time partners with Moss, weren't you?" Carberry's voice had grown sharper, more acid and cutting. He snapped the cruiser into drive; they lurched forward, away from the curb. "Yeah, that's your whole trouble, Dan, I figure it now. Ol' Monk was enough to bugger up any normal man."

The pure contempt startled Brashear enough to make him turn and look again at Carberry. In the luminous green glow of the dashboard light, the face had a stiff and brittle deadness to it, the cruel remark fitting it quite naturally. And as he watched Carberry, it slowly dawned on Brashear what Moss had been

Judas Cross

essentially concerned with all along. There are no differences in compromise, only various degrees of it. He couldn't understand why the truth had suddenly come, only that it had and that it was, and that up until now, he had been defending a myth. He was as ignorant in his own dishonesty as Carberry was in his, and it mattered naught which was the greater. To face Carberry was to face himself, a mirror of delusion and corruption.

He glanced away once more, out at the deserted street. He studied the empty houses and silent stores, ignoring his partner beside him; it was all emptiness and silence, including Carberry. But to accuse Carberry of failing as a cop and as a man and not himself would mean he had some idea of an answer, and he had none. He had nothing but pain, a pain for which he could not find the source. Damn Moss, damn him and his moral outrage. It was almost as if the dead man *were* returning, somehow resurrecting in his head. And it was damnable Mossam Turnbeau who was now dredging up that abysmal quote; it had to be, because Brashear was too lousy at literature to recall more than nursery rhymes, but crazy or not, there it was, billowing full-grown out of some musty ash can of collegiate memory, going round and round in the torment of his mind:

Think of us, not as lost, violent souls,
But only as hollow men, the stuffed men,

If the hour should strike for me as it struck for him,
Nothing I possess could save me . . .

2-f

"Contractor bought out the Emerson farm," his father said. "Only a couple of weeks ago, and already they've cleared the land, getting ready to put up a passel of matchboxes."

"That's a shame. Emerson get a good price?"

"I don't know, he's gone to Florida. Not that I blame him any. It's getting awfully cluttered around here."

They were standing under a walnut tree on the rim of the hill. Wind shivered through the branches and made waves in the fields below, a tide of tall grass with spume of white seed. The gray-green earth beckoned skyward like a woman's arms; they were alone on the hill save for the house at the bottom. It was his father's house, his grandfather's before that, square and white as if freshly painted, contained by a low stone wall and a strip of garden. In summer the stone was lichen-yellow while the garden blossomed. Now the stone was gray and the garden dead, and there was desolation among the weeds.

"Seems everybody is moving here to get away from it all," his father said, "and bringing it right along with them. I read in the paper about your partner. Turnbeau, wasn't he?"

"That's right, Moss Turnbeau."

"Thought so. Hell of a thing, to be gunned like that. I remember Finney saying he carried a pistol so he could be around to go to church the next Sunday, but I don't think he ever used it. I don't think there was one fellow killed, whole time I was on the force."

Brashear looked down at the house. He had lived there most of his life, most of his twenty-eight years to the day, and he knew it by heart: the creak of the walls, the peace of the cellar, the smell of earth that lingered forever. "A city's a sour place, Dad, a lot different than up here."

"Oh, I don't know. We had our days, mostly during Pro-hi. There was the time we raided the Hawaiian Resort, just this side of Rochester. I don't know if you recall Sam Lucarto, he died when you were five or six, I guess, but he sold a right mean product. Gennie Scotch Whiskey, blended from straight alcohol and the right tint of maple, and bottled in the original Karo Syrup jar. You could always tell his customers by the red creases across the bridge of their noses."

He chuckled with memory, and for no particular reason, stooped to pull at a dandelion. "And then there was the duck farm, so neat each coop had the same amount of dirt and feathers in it. Made us curious, so we pried up the boards. Found a hundred-and-fifty-gallon still and its owner training a rifle on

Judas Cross

us. But we never lost a man, Daniel, not a one. How's his widow faring?"

"Not too well. I haven't seen her since the funeral, and she was . . . pretty broken up then."

Out came the root, making a crater beside the path. "Does she blame you, son?"

Brashear studied his father for a moment, seeing the wind pluck at his thinning white hair, the coat of muddy soil on his shoes, the creases of his fingers as they clutched the unwanted plant. They were coarse, calloused hands, stained with labor and tobacco on their palms and tips. They had always been so, from before his father had retired, from before he could recollect them holding him as a child.

"Yes," he said, and his voice was one with the wind.

"Guess that's only natural. She'll get over it. Haven't you found a trace of the killer yet? This man who was staying at some motel with a girl?"

"Yes, and we're holding him. He's not the killer, though."

"Oh? I knew you're after him, but I must've missed that part."

"Probably the papers didn't cover it, you know how they lose interest once the blood's mopped up. We've a couple of minor charges against him, but he's got a solid alibi for that night."

"So who else have you got?"

"That's the rub. Schmidt and Nalisco have been beating their—"

"Who?"

"Schmidt and Nalisco, they're the ones handling the case."

"What about you?"

"What about me?"

"He was your partner, wasn't he?"

"Moss was partners with 'most everybody at one time or another. A team was assigned, same as for any other homicide in Portlawn, and I happen not to be on it."

"But you're a cop."

"Sure I'm a cop," Brashear said, stiffening. "And I've got

my own assignments to work on. Just what's that supposed to mean?"

"Just that. You're a cop."

"And they are too, and they're both good men. They want the killer as much as I do."

"All right, you're not a cop," his father said just as stubbornly, and flung the weed away.

Down at the house, the back door opened and Brashear's mother stepped outside, ringing an old cow bell. It was too far to see her distinctly, but he knew she was ringing it the way she always had, arm flailing as if the elbow were loose. The bell made a dull, hollow sound which sent an autumnal bird winging from the grass, only to settle again when the door was shut.

"Hope you're hungry, birthday boy. She's been grieving all morning over that cake of yours."

Brashear tugged his coat collar higher around his neck, the gusts harsher as they stepped from the shelter of the tree and started down the path. The grass was swollen with last night's rain, quivering with crystal pearls when brushed against—quivering with a fitfulness which matched Brashear's own impatient wandering of the hill with his father. He had been trying to find some emotional stability since finishing his shift with Carberry; something solid to touch with his mind even as his reasoning decried the possibility. Failing, his restlessness had lengthened with the afternoon, growing as he watched the shadows darken the house and crust the empty fish pond. Yet, he still searched as though to seek his elusive clue among them, the shadows seeming to subdue all except himself.

Brashear kept his mouth shut until they had reached the flagstone porch. Then, impulsively, he turned on his father. "What was that last crack for? The one about not being a cop?"

His father paused to scrape a ball of mud from his shoe, breathless from exertion or reluctance, Brashear couldn't tell which. "I remember," he said at last, "how you used to play with my white gloves and shiny buttons. And how I used to tell you there was more to a policeman than a uniform."

"Oh, and you think I'm shirking responsibilities, is that it?"

"You've got a duty, like it or not."

"You don't think I like it the way it is, do you? My lieutenant ordered me to stay strictly off the investigation, or face suspension. It's not that I won't—I *can't* do anything."

"Maybe so, maybe so." He sounded terribly weary right then. "I've a few beliefs that can't be exchanged when they're inconvenient. I'm too old and I've carried them around with me too long for that. Don't condemn me for having them, son."

"Condemn you? *You're* the one condemning *me.* You talk of duty, but I've got a duty to my superiors to obey orders, and to my wife not to get fired. What choice do I have? Come on, Dad, be sensible."

"The Original Sin," he murmured, opening the back door.

"What?"

"The dogma of man losing his vision by chasing the practicalities of this world." Not in anger, but tired and sad, the older man made a sweeping gesture across the land they'd just walked. "Consider the lilies of the field," he said, and went inside.

Brashear followed him into the house, feeling there was little he could respond to that. The interior smelled crisp of roast beef and cinnamon of home-canned fruit. His father retired down the hall to the bathroom. Brashear was left to pace the parquetry of the dining room and moodily study the rose-bud wallpaper, the tasseled lace curtains, the thick oak table in the center, extended and covered with a white cloth. On the table were bowls of beans and potatoes, a platter of sliced French bread of sorts, and underneath a silver dome that had been new about the turn of the century, a three-cornered rump roast the way he loved it, more garlic than meat.

Valerie backed through the swinging door, laden with plates, and from the other side came the kitchen bustle of one old lady and one very much younger lady showing each other how to cook. Valerie was wearing a salmon-colored sleeveless dress Brashear had never cared for much, but he enjoyed the way it pulled like pink flesh over her tightened breasts when she leaned over the table. She stacked the dishes at the head end, straightened and pressed back a wisp of stray hair with her hand.

"We'd thought you'd gotten lost out there. Ready for dinner?"

"Soon's I wash."

"Where's your father?"

"In the bathroom. That's why I'm waiting."

"Use the kitchen sink, then," his mother said, entering. "The bathroom is his hibernatorium." She had thin, corded wrists and ankles, and was dressed in a woolen suit she'd bought in Canada a decade before and would never wear out. Her hair was softly gray and cropped short to accentuate its natural curliness. There was an honesty about her, a strength and honesty wrapped in a tiny body. She was carrying her own separate dinner—no fat, no salt; what a way to have to eat.

"That looks terrible," Brashear said, inspecting the blah food. "You deserve better than that on my birthday."

"My doctor heard that, he'd have a fit. Now, go wash."

When Brashear returned from the kitchen, his father was sitting at the head of the table. He took the chair at the opposite end; his mother was on his right, Valerie and Lisa together on his left. His father lifted the silver lid and began carving the roast, ignoring him. Brashear stared coldly at his silverware, an emptiness inside him, the same emptiness which had been draining him for days now.

Valerie placed a comforting hand on his arm. "Smile a little, dear. What are you so grouchy about?"

"Nothing." Brashear glanced at Valerie, and suddenly the remainder of his patience vanished. "Nothing but the usual. Your father-in-law does not wish his son to be a cop, not now or ever."

"That's right," his father replied evenly. He passed a plate. "I don't think you've the guts to be one. I've always felt business would have suited you better."

Brashear stared rigidly at his wife for a moment longer, as if for support. But Valerie was as silent as he, head bowed slightly in embarrassment. Sure, he thought savagely, she would be quiet now. She'd been full of it all the way up from Portlawn—think of your job, think of my position, think of Lisa, of all the social and financial arguments she could muster for not rocking

Judas Cross

the boat. But she'd little-talked herself empty. He was alone. The frustration and pain inside him continued to peel away his nerves, until finally he regarded his father with cold resentment, his words sharp fragments of bitterness.

"Guts? What kind of guts? The guts it takes to raid a duck farm?"

"Exactly, the guts to raid a duck farm. There's been a lot of that in my life, son, things I wouldn't have wished on another human being but which had to be done. Lord only knows how many men curse me to this day, but I know one who never has. Me. I have yet to curse my own soul."

"Stop this," his mother said tersely. "I'm sure Daniel feels bad enough as it is."

"Not yet, but he might get that way eventually."

"Just what the hell are you trying to do to me, anyway?"

"Not I, son. The devil is made in one's own image."

"Oh, that's lovely. That's beautiful. Is that your own?"

"I doubt it. Most originality is merely new mixtures of old ideas."

"There's another one. You've been talking profoundly ever since we got here, vast platitudes that don't mean a damn thing. Explain, will you?"

His father laid the carving knife gently aside. "It would only be an echo."

The old man paused, feeling withered and useless, shamed at the gulf between him and his son. He fought it within himself, his expression set but his hands shaking slightly, determined that though he couldn't seem to make Daniel understand, he would at least refuse to betray him further. Noticing his hands, he abruptly clasped them together and lowered his head. "Let us say grace . . ."

The phone rang, interrupting the prayer. Brashear's mother answered it, returning to say, "It's long distance for you, Daniel."

Brashear excused himself, sick and heavy and grateful for the reprieve. He was gone a long time. When he came back he was trembling, and in an effort to keep the tremor from his voice, he spoke carefully, succinctly.

"That was Lenin, on day watch. He thought I'd like to know."

"Yes?"

"They caught the killer."

2-g

Silence was spoken loudest of all.

Viscid traffic crept southward through the Catskills, among leaves dulled and fallen along the wayside. The surrounding hills were old women's breasts, spreading bleak and depleted against a twilight wash of indifferent gray. The mood of the earth, the sky, of Brashear was depressed and muted. Even Lisa, perched on the back seat in her sticky red boots, seemed curiously somber as they returned to Portlawn.

Brashear's stomach was thick with birthday cake and his father's pressing disapproval. It had not slackened with Lenin's call, there now being disdain for a son not in on the capture. And leaden satire: Got the right guy now? No mistake this time, Billie Dee Adam is the killer?

No mistake, according to Lenin.

Billie Dee Adam: self-styled local radical without a pot to piss in, claiming the Black Panthers were soft on Whitey after they'd refused him membership. Brashear had only sketchy details from his conversation with Lenin, but evidently it had been the search of the files which had unearthed him. Billie Dee had once threatened in court to gut Turnbeau for having arrested him. That had been years ago and he was out on parole now, but you know how them black bastards from East Portlawn never forget. Yeah, and a rifle had been found in his car when he'd been picked up for questioning. His alibi had boomeranged; the four men with whom he'd allegedly been at the time of Moss's death had, after two hours of careful reconsideration, denied he'd shown up until midnight. He'd called them liars, among other things, but it was his word against theirs. The logical route for him to have taken to their

Judas Cross

apartment was along Laurentide, past the Bideewee. Through the two-way glass of the interrogation room, Arlen Hilton had identified Adam as the man seen running past his house. Being warehouseman for LePage Electronic Supply Company, Billie Dee could've even been aware that Quaker had visited there two weeks before. Though how that fit, if at all, Lenin had failed to explain over the phone.

But everything considered, the day crew had whipped together a credible, if circumstantial, case against him. According to Lenin, Billie Dee had chanced upon Turnbeau at the stakeout, and seen his chance for revenge and notoriety. Not that he'd confessed, not his kind who grovel for recognition, and the shotgun had yet to be found, if ever. But no mollycoddling court was going to let him off this time, so he could hijack a plane to Coobah or something. No mistake; that Commie nigrah revolootionary was grabbed by the chandaliers.

Despite the favorable news, Brashear continued to feel restive, a discontent etching his features sullen. He drove with exaggerated care, intent upon another's sudden braking, an accidental swerve, the abrupt incaution, wishing for silence because he couldn't concentrate with a lot of idle chatter going on. What he really wished was to be by himself.

"Are you going out later, dear?"

"What?"

"I said, are you planning to go out later, to the station?"

They were nearing their house, on Frenchtown Avenue now, just before Wiletta Lane. Brashear glanced at his wife beside him, saw the tensed curve of her body, the turbulence in her eyes as if they were stirred by something she could not understand. She didn't want him to go out.

"It's my night off," he said. "Why should I?"

"I thought after the phone call you might want to."

"Lenin was just passing on what's happened, that's all. Christ, can't you get it through your head any better than my father that this is not my case? I've nothing to do with it."

"You don't have to snap at me, Dan."

At length he said, "I don't know. I might, for a minute or two."

Moodiness followed him after he parked. He stood on the sidewalk in front of their house, hands in his pockets, watching his wife and daughter get out of the car. He remained unaware of the battered sports car across the street, or of the girl who climbed out of it, until she called to him.

"Detective Brashear? Are you Detective Brashear?"

Brashear, too surly to be startled, turned slowly and gazed at the girl. She was black; not only Negro, but black black, a charcoal posture against the evening. She waved an arm at him energetically. "Don't go, I want to talk to you."

She crossed Wiletta with quick, angular movements. Brashear was surprised to find her, as she neared, become more of a woman than her profile had first indicated. She was short, like a girl; tiny-breasted and heavy-hipped, the way a girl can be during puberty; and her hair was drawn back in a braidlike affair more common to girls than to full-grown women. She was wearing a short, loose shift of tartan plaid, and her legs looked cold. Yet her face was mature, modeled of delicate bone, and when she stood in front of Brashear, the little-girl image entirely disappeared. Her gray, deliberate eyes held a hard adult intensity.

"I'm Kitt Rainey," she said, setting a scuffed leather briefcase down on the sidewalk. "I've been appointed to represent Mr. Adam. I'm sorry to have—"

"You?"

Her eyes grew almost reptilian. "What is it—my skin or my sex?"

"Neither." Brashear was momentarily nonplused. "Or maybe both together, that and your age. You look too young to be a lawyer."

"I'm not. I'm twenty-five, most of which was spent getting away from East Portlawn. But you're right in that I'm not fully accredited yet; I'm a fourth-year student at New York University, working as a volunteer for the Wilcox Committee to get experience."

"How nice," Valerie said. "I used to go to N.Y.U."

Brashear rubbed his forehead. "Val, where's Lisa?"

"Here"—from underfoot.

Judas Cross

"Take her inside, Val." He paused, and when nothing happened, added sternly, "Now, Val." He kept looking at Kitt Rainey, seeing her stiffen when he'd spoken to his wife, and after Valerie had hustled their daughter as far as the porch, he said, "You don't approve of that either, I take it."

"No, but I'm here for Mr. Adam, not Fem Lib."

"All the way from New York for him?"

Her reply was edged. "We've lots of work in Portlawn."

"You sound like we're nothing but rednecks here."

"I told you, I came from Portlawn. We lived over the Purple Cow, on Straight. I remember you cops coming down the block in your trucks, rounding up everybody like we were cattle, herding us through the station to see what you could pin on us. I remember the riots of '63. Don't tell me what it's like here."

"I wouldn't think to, miss."

"And don't tell me there isn't work to do. You know the system in this state: a court-appointed lawyer earns the same fee whether he defends his client or pleads him guilty. So he pleads him guilty whether he is or not. That isn't justice."

"You're very idealistic."

"Maybe, but which is worse—an idealistic student willing to fight for her client, or an experienced lawyer who isn't?"

"I'm sure I don't know."

Her face eased some of its flaring anger. "I don't know either. Lord, there are times I don't know either."

"Well, while you're figuring it out, I'm going inside."

"Wait! Wait a minute, will you?" Her voice was pained and exhausted. "I . . . shouldn't have climbed onto my soapbox that way. It's been an exasperating day for me."

"It has been for me, too. Good night, Miss Rainey."

"Please, listen to me. A man's life may depend on it."

"Oh, come on. Billie Dee's?"

"Yes, Billie Dee's. Even Billie Dee's."

"He's a nothing, a nobody, he shotgunned my partner. I leave it to you to shed any tears."

"Maybe he didn't kill him."

"That's for the courts to decide."

"Then who're you to tell me he did and walk away?"

There was one of those fractured moments of silence while Brashear rubbed his forehead some more, then lower, down around the sockets of his tired eyes. He wondered vaguely if he was coming down with a headache. "Miss Rainey, what do you want?"

"Want? I want to *know,* that's what I want. I want to be convinced of his innocence or his guilt, so I can best advise him. And I want some cooperation, though that seems to be impossible. Those four men, for example, the ones he was supposedly with that night. They looked at me like I didn't exist and denied everything."

"Don't sound so disgusted. Billie Dee tried to grow an alibi for a cop killing. What do you expect them to do but fold?"

"Have you talked with them?"

"No, I'm going by what I've heard."

"They've been leaned on. Hard. 'Don't go stirring soup, missie, not for the likes of Billie Dee.' And another told me, 'I have to live here, there's something for nothing.'"

Brashear shrugged. "They're that kind."

"Like all *nigrahs?*"

"I see you've been talking to Sergeant Lenin. You'll have to excuse him; he's from South Jersey. But no, trash comes in assorted colors."

"And Arlen Hilton? Do marshmallows come other than white?"

"Why d'you say that?"

"I've been to see him, too. Only he locked the door on me, looked as if I were a monster or something. But I've read his statement, the original one he gave the day after the murder. His description then was of an average man wearing casual clothes. Does Arlen Hilton strike you as being so unprejudiced that when he sees Negro, he doesn't see black?"

"He was highly upset at the time. It could have occurred to him later, when he faced Billie Dee."

"Or was he persuaded? A little urging, that kind of gentle brainwashing which made your line-up illegal? 'We know he's guilty, Mr. Hilton,'" she said, lowering her voice. "'We've got the evidence, and all we need is your identification to wrap it up.

Judas Cross

He's the one, isn't he? Say so, and you'll clear the streets of another dangerous killer.' "

"Well, that's something *you* don't know, Miss Rainey." Brashear, soured of her antagonism on top of the rest of the day, was curt and impatient. "You've been knocking me and my profession pretty freely, and I could stay and argue police procedure and civil rights, but I'm not going to. I'm going in to the two women I keep in domestic slave labor and beat for fun and pleasure. And you're going to go away now because I can't help you or Billie Dee. I've been out of town and don't know what went on, and there's no reason I should, because I'm not involved."

"You're not involved?" It came from the back of her throat. "You're not involved? What do you call your report if not being involved?"

"What about my report?"

"You were there, you saw what happened."

"I—" He snapped his mouth shut on the truth.

"You described Mr. Adam almost down to his name—beard, granny glasses, long hair, Castro-type uniform. And you didn't miss that he was black, as Mr. Hilton did, even from twenty yards away. How can you be anything except involved?"

"This was all in my report?"

"I admit that of the witnesses, you're the most damaging, and I should wait until after you've faced him, but—" She stopped to eye Brashear with a new, acute intensity. "Will you give an honest identification, or am I being too naïve?"

"You're sure you read it correctly?"

She blinked as if slightly confused. "Of course I did. I saw all the evidence against Mr. Adam. Why? Is there something I missed?"

"No, no . . ." Brashear contemplated the night Moss died and what he'd written of it, and a snake crawled up his spine and clutched at his throat. "Look, Miss Rainey, it's late, and there's nothing I can do for you tonight. I'm not sure there is at all. Your arguments are with the DA, or with the men handling the investigation, not with me."

"In other words, you're washing your hands, and I made a fat mistake by talking to you."

"You didn't and I'm not. I put it badly. You've been unorthodox, but we could probably use more of it, and maybe something will come of it. In a sense you're being naïve; either you don't have to ask, or it won't do you any good to. But believe me, it wasn't a mistake."

"I'm going to see you again."

"I can't stop you." He managed to smile; it was tight, distant with preoccupation. "I'll be . . . fair with Billie Dee."

He stared morosely while Kitt Rainey recrossed the street. His snake had fangs and blood pounded in his temples, the headache very real. He stood in silence a long moment more, then strode swiftly up to the door of his house.

"She's nuts," he muttered. "She's made it all up." The girl was gone, but her words lingered on. He opened the door and called inside: "Valerie, I'm going out . . ."

Brashear hoped Lenin would still be at the precinct station, but by the time he arrived, the shifts had changed and most of the day watch had left, including Lenin. His bunch was on: Fratelli reading *A Mother's Love* in the muster room; Robard BS-ing with Handall of the day watch and with Pantages, the banjo-eyed regular sent from Metro's Burglary Detail to fill Moss's vacancy; Carberry catching because it was Brashear's night off; Nalisco and Schmidt looking smug after having booked Adam in the Sanponset County Jail. The looie's door was ajar, indicating he was around. The station moved in methodical, inexorable routine no matter who was on duty, and normally Brashear would have felt a reassurance, a comfort and a pride at being part of this familiar, flowing system. Now he found himself at odds with it.

"Who wrote this?" he demanded.

"You did," Schmidt said, and looked foxy.

"Shit," Brashear said. He was standing by the filing cabinets, a carbon of his Supplementary Report DD5 gripped in his hand. His features were lean, drawn in around his mouth, his dark eyes piercing and more distinct. "I mean it. Handall? You were here then. Who wrote this?"

Judas Cross

Everybody looked at Handall, and Handall inspected the ceiling.

"You did," Schmidt repeated after a pause, becoming terse in reaction to Brashear's anger. "What's the bitch? You want to retract it?"

"I want to know who rewrote it and then had the balls to sign my name to it."

"Let it lie, Dan."

"Hell I will. It's got me down as witnessing Adam shoot Moss that night, don't you understand?"

"I understand a cheap bohunk thought he could swing a cop killing," Handall interjected, sharp and caustic. "I understand he ain't laughing out his ass no more. That I understand. Only I don't understand your objection."

"Who wrote this thing!"

The door to the inner office opened and Lieutenant Jules came out. He was holding a nearly empty glass of milk and wore a white mustache on the upper lip of his pursed mouth. "What is this? What's all this shouting?" He glared around his squad room, spotted Brashear and asked, "What are you doing here?" and when there was no immediate response, he said, "Come into my office, Brashear."

He left the door wide and went back behind his desk, setting the glass down on a pile of papers. He slumped in his chair, took off his hat and looked around as if wondering where to place it, then put it back on. The small refrigerator beneath the one window started, vibrating the Venetian-blind sash resting on its top. He glanced at it, then opened the refrigerator and refilled his glass from a half-gallon carton, right to the rim.

"Like a barometer," he said, closing the refrigerator. "Higher I keep my milk, the more my ulcer is grinding. Have you seen the *Record* today?"

"No, sir."

Brashear, having followed the lieutenant and shut the door, sat in the office's straight-backed chair. He could hear his nerves screaming. He had the peculiar feeling that he was being led up to something that wouldn't be the truth. At least not the whole truth, but a placation, a glossing over of the forgery for the sake of expediency before it was hastily discarded. It left him with a sense of being used.

"Damn newspaper's been killing us," Lieutenant Jules went on. "Been calling us incompetent and crooks ever since Turnbeau died. Thank God that's over and we got the guy who did it, right?"

"You got him with this?" Brashear said, and slapped the phony report down on the desk.

The lieutenant placed a hand over his pained stomach. "No, not exactly."

"Why was it used?"

"Well, I don't think it should have been, but I wasn't here when they dreamed it up. I can't blame the boys too much; this Billie Dee Adam is hard as rock, and they were using everything to soften him up, get him jugged before he could skip town. They thought they could wave this under his nose as a clincher, get him to break."

"He didn't."

"He doesn't have a chance anyway, Brashear. The report won't have to be used again; by the time we reach preliminary hearing, all the loopholes will be blocked. He'll have copped a plea by then. He knows he doesn't have a defense."

"Four friends could change their minds again."

"They won't, you can count on that. And who's going to believe him otherwise? He's got a package going back to when he was twelve—stealing gloves, assaulting an officer, a couple of D&D's; the last one when Moss collared him was for auto theft. He's scum, Brashear! Be reasonable!"

"You think his lawyer will be?"

"Oh, her."

"Yes, her. She's not about to let him plead guilty if she can help it. That would be too easy for her."

"Bad as those pesky lap dogs, always nipping at your heels."

"Well, she has a damn big trainer. Or did you know she was working under the Wilcox Commission?"

"For chrissake, no! How did you?"

"She came to see me, that's how I heard about this in the

first place. You think they'll be reasonable when they discover evidence has been faked?"

"They won't find out."

"How can they help it? She's on a crusade; she'll question it as soon as the DA doesn't present your so-called clincher. And what happens if I appear?"

"Exactly why you weren't supposed to know."

"Well, I do. I can't testify; it'll blow the case against him."

"I don't see why . . ."

"Sir, this isn't the same as . . . as fudging the truth over a traffic ticket."

The lieutenant avoided looking at him, sipping his milk with even, measured swallows. "I'm well aware of that. I don't like this any better than you do, but what's done is done, there's no way to undo the damage."

Brashear felt a sickness contract the back of his throat. "But if my testimony should convict Billie Dee, sir . . ."

"Think of my squad out there, of *your* squad, and how it would ruin the department if you turned against us. What's important now is for us, all of us, to stick together as a team, right?"

"But the courts, sir, if they uphold this new amendment, the one with the mandatory death sentence for killing policemen . . ."

The eyes bulged, the voice a rasp. "Dammit, then think of yourself, if nobody else! We soft-pedaled your dereliction at the motel, but your career will be finished if it is made public. This way lets you off the hook, could even bring you a citation!"

Brashear had never before been in conflict with Lieutenant Jules, had never questioned a decision or argued a reprimand. His face grew pale, squeezed, tortured-looking.

"*Right?*"

"Yes . . . sir."

"That's better. If I were you, Brashear, I wouldn't be so eager to look a gift horse in the mouth."

Brashear rose and opened the door as if dismissed. He walked through the squad room, a vacant feeling between his shoulder blades, reluctant to submit and afraid to refuse. If it should come to court, it would mean another compromise, one that would save himself and the rest of the men. What was Billie Dee in comparison? None of the others would hesitate if faced with this choice of survival. None but Moss, perhaps.

And Moss was dead.

He went down the stairs two at a time as though pursued, his mind groping around the dilemma from both its sides. There had to be more than two; there had to be another way besides either/or . . .

Kitt Rainey was at the muster desk, berating Fratelli. Christ no, not this too, not now. He tried to brush past her, but she turned and plucked the sleeve of his arm.

"Help me," she said.

Brashear looked at her despairingly. "What now, Miss Rainey?"

"I'm trying to get a doctor for Mr. Adam."

"There's one at the jail."

She laughed with cynicism. "He's only interested in telling dirty jokes to see if I'll blush."

"What's the matter with Billie Dee?" he asked Fratelli.

Fratelli shrugged, relieved that the girl was pestering somebody else. "They sent her over here, I don't know why. Nothing we can do."

"Have you seen him yet?" she asked Brashear.

"No."

"I was at the jail when he was booked in; believe me, he needs a doctor. I can't seem to get one short of a court order, and that may take forever. You can get into his cellblock, do something for him."

"I'm on duty."

"No, you're not."

There was a short, brittle pause. Brashear started for the entrance again. " 'Night, Fratelli."

"Yo."

Kitt tagged after him. "Don't you care? You put him there."

"I did not! I didn't arrest him, did I?"

"Your evidence did." She repeated stubbornly, "You put him there."

"Go away, Miss Rainey!"

"You promised to see Mr. Adam anyway. You might as well while you can do some good for him."

"God! All right, I'll see him! Anything your heart desires, only leave me alone for a while!" He stood on the wide front steps, filled with an insane compulsion to throttle her, the whole thing overwhelming him.

"Why are you staring that way?"

"What?"

"Up there, at the crest on the wall."

Brashear tried to pass it off lightly, as if a joke. "To see if it's going to fall down and hit me, I guess."

"Not a bad idea. There's nothing but decay holding it up . . ."

He drove the three minutes to the jail, furious with the whole idea. It'd first occurred to him on the stairs; he'd forced it from his mind after one flickering instant. He'd hated it more while Kitt Rainey was goading him into agreement, and now a portion of his loathing was directed inward, toward his capitulation and rout. What was he *doing*, going to see this man? The best he could hope for was that by facing Adam, he'd become intuitively convinced of his guilt and feel no pain should a compromise become necessary. Somehow, even that had the smell of a trap worth avoiding.

He parked, checked his pistol at the booking desk, and accompanied one of the guards, Zinzer, to the elevator. Zinzer was five years older than Brashear but already larded, myopic and balding; whenever they were together, Brashear was reminded of how transitory flesh is. Then he'd listen to the jingle of Zinzer's keys, and look at the drab-gray metal sides of the elevator with their welded eyelets in which to snap handcuffs, and he'd be reminded of the immortality which is jailhouse life.

Sanponset County Jail was circa 1954, one of the newer buildings in Portlawn, and certainly one of the newest joints in Jersey. It backsided busy Carlington Avenue, with a little bordering park so as not to offend any passing traffic. The entrance was around on Bedford, the next street parallel, and had a parking strip, three large doors for delivery, a first floor of unbarred windows, and three more floors of pale brick and frosted-glass cubes. It didn't look a jail; it looked the model of corporate respectability in an otherwise sleazy neighborhood.

But inside, Sanponset County Jail was exactly what it was supposed to be: a holding pen. It held you if you had a year's sentence or less, or were in transit between court and prison, or couldn't make bail, or if the few cells in Portlawn's municipal jug were full and there wasn't any place else to put you. A few of the longer-term trustees worked in the kitchen, which was a cushy deal, since it allowed you to eat something besides Kix and powdered milk for breakfast. If you weren't in the kitchen, you were in your cell from eight to six, or you sat on your fud in a 50 by 75 day cage, one per each block of six four-man cells. You sat on your fud with last week's newspaper or last month's letter or last year's paperback, and you waited. You waited for a new arrival, a new story, for something to happen to confirm you were still awake and functioning. Prisons aged you double-quick; county jails held you in limbo.

What Sanponset really was, Brashear thought, was a time machine.

Billie Dee Adam was on the third floor, left wing, first block, for no particular reason other than that's where an empty bunk had been. The men were in the day cage, waiting for the first lights-out bell to send them to their cells—lights-out being a misnomer, since they merely dimmed a little. That's how night and day were told, by lamps and bells, though on a really sunny day, the frosted-glass cubes were brighter than the concrete walls.

Zinzer called out, "Adam!"

The men stirred with ruminative apathy.

Zinzer yelled through the tool-proof steel bars, "Billie Adam!"

"In cell Five," one of the men finally said. "Thorenson let him lay down there."

"Go get him, Pacelli, and be quick about it."

The man called Pacelli got up grudgingly from his bench. Zinzer inserted a key into the control stand and pushed a couple of buttons. Cell door 5 and the door to the cell corridor shot back with a din. Brashear, at the near end of the corridor, slipped his arms through the bars and rested them on a crosspiece, his fingers nervously jiggling a small box of Red Devil Beard Depilatory he'd found sitting there.

Pacelli came out of cell 5, dwarfed under the Negro he was supporting, while Adam, swollen head lolling, tried to work spaghetti legs. Pacelli forced him to walk to Brashear, then left him there to return to the day cage, his face clamped in a resentment his mouth knew better than to voice. Adam was dressed, as they all were, in soft, faded-blue dungarees and work shirt, only his had dark stains dribbled down the front. He didn't look up at first, but seemed to gradually become aware. When he did, his blotched face had a foul nakedness to it despite the beard and long hair, and his eyes, Brashear saw, were so bloodshot that there were hardly any whites. He was missing his glasses.

"Hey," he managed. "No more problems, hey?"

"I just want to go over a few things," Brashear said.

"That's what leads to them problems."

Zinzer, having relocked the doors, came up beside Brashear. "Get him to tell you how he shot Turnbeau."

"No way, Mister Man. I didn't know he was around. Hey, like I was someplace else, someplace long gone from there."

Brashear turned to the guard. "What happened to him?"

"We got him this way," Zinzer replied indifferently. "He must've had one of those accidents on the way over."

Brashear looked at Adam again, a wretchedness growing inside of him. He forced his voice to remain objective. "Listen, where were you that night?"

"Makes no diff, Mister Man."

"It might."

"Ever happen to you, you go out with your friends, only the next day they don't remember you were along? Like you didn't exist for them? Ever happen to you?"

"No."

"Not before to me, neither. Gets to me, hey. Gets me thinking maybe I don't remember right no more. Gets my head hurting. It don't feel so good, all the time making me thirsty."

"There's water in your cell," Zinzer said.

"Can't work it right. Can't push the button and hold my finger to the spout both the same time. Can't get it to shoot up."

"Can you find him a cup?" Brashear asked the guard.

Zinzer looked affronted. "If I had to."

"Hey, no help. Any more your kind of help, and you'll need a shovel. You're all invited to the burial."

"That's a mighty fat lip you've got, Billie."

"Billie *Dee*." Adam used the bars to straighten himself in front of Zinzer. "I'm Billie Dee and I live fat, too."

"Sure, take a good look around you."

"Temp-orary, Mister Man."

"Don't make book on it."

"Got a problem, get Billie Dee. He says he didn't do it, he's lying. You made me fall once, and figure I'll roll over for anything else, but uh-uh. Not this time." Adam began to slump, eyes closing and belly pumping from the exertion of his breathing. "I'll get out. Somebody'll believe me. Somebody's got to."

Brashear saw the pulp of his mouth and the perspiration that beaded his forehead, and wondered how high his temperature was. "Easy," he said. "Take it easy, Billie Dee."

"Billie Dee, that's my name. I didn't know no bull was there. I didn't know nobody was nowhere, did you?"

"Get the doctor down here," Brashear told Zinzer.

"What for? For him?"

"Billie Dee, that's my name, and I live fat too. I could sure use a little drink."

"For Christ's sake, he's half delirious!"

Zinzer scowled. "A few days on the floor, and he'll be okay."

Brashear stared at the guard, his shirt cold and sticking to his back. Zinzer wavered and faded from view. Turnbeau appeared instead, he and the ghost of expediency; and Brashear's father with practicality; and an idealistic student so inured to Portlawn cops, she hadn't bothered to complain that her client had been beaten, but only pleaded for a doctor.

Judas Cross

He heard Adam say, "A doctor, hey sweet charity. Keep it up; when the time comes I'll save you a place."

And Zinzer: "Only thing he needs is a little more face lifting."

It snapped, then, a spontaneous bursting in his head that shattered reality down on him. "Adam's being rammed through tomorrow or the next day," he lied, and could've bitten his tongue but kept on lying. "He's got to be in condition to appear in court. How's it going to look if we show him drooling at the mouth and unable to walk?"

"Well, why didn't you say so?" Zinzer retorted. "Why don't we get told these things around here?"

"I am, now! Get the doctor, will you?"

Adam focused briefly on Brashear and attempted to grin, though the left side of his face was peculiarly slack. "Mister Man, you're going to make one hell of a father-in-law."

3-a

Brashear did not go home, nor did he return to the station after leaving the jail. He sat in his car and shook.

He'd blown it.

And yet he knew intuitively that if he'd been able to do it over, he'd have called the doctor sooner. What had failed to penetrate him on a logical level had finally succeeded on an emotional one. He'd been broken, crushed, but in the troubled depths of his deeper self, Brashear recognized it was far from finished. It was obvious to him that were he forced to testify in court, he would not lie. He *could* not lie, it was that simple. As through a glass darkly, he saw now that there was only one direction left for him, a single course open for a man to take.

Find the truth.

Somehow find it, and damn the lieutenant. He'd taken the first step by seeing Adam, but now where to continue, what to try?

A whisper of a thought. Brashear strained to catch it. But it was drowned by his new compulsion, still tangled and confused. Plans and methods occurred to him; he rejected each as impractical or a waste of time. He could interrogate the four men with whom Adam had been, but they'd answer yes or no depending on the strength and direction of the wind. He could retrace the investigation, but Schmidt and Nalisco had been efficient and thorough, ending up with Billie Dee and some weak circumstantial evidence. He doubted he'd do any better. Another tack had to be taken, and the ghost of that first thought returned, haunting him by its very elusiveness. It refused to form, obstinately pale. It was a nothing, and yet . . .

He started the car, reversing swiftly from the parking strip. It wasn't quite eight o'clock; she'd be home by now. She might not want to talk to him, or if she did, he wasn't sure that she could help, but still . . . Still the idea persisted, gradually solidifying as he drove across town.

The house on Poplar had just that, a poplar tall and narrow in the yard. The house was russet-colored, with a steep slate-surfaced roof and pillared front, and had come, Brashear recalled, from a Sears, Roebuck catalog. A 1928 do-it-yourself home, five rooms and a bath, furnished, ready-cut and fitted, just pound the nails (included). There'd been a succession of owners, but still it looked sturdy. The nails had been pounded well. The upper section of the front door had a glass panel, and through its white net curtain enough light shone to illuminate the three iron geese which paraded near the steps. Brashear glanced at the geese as he walked to the door; they looked as if they were trying to escape.

Soft, whispery conversation seemed to come from inside the house, but when Moss Turnbeau's widow answered his knock, there was nothing but silence behind her.

"Hello, Flo."

Her eyes were lifeless voids; the eyes of a dead woman.

"Am I interrupting anything?"

Her voice matched her eyes. "What's there to interrupt?"

"I . . . thought you might not be alone."

"I am, very. Come in."

They went down a short hall to the parlor. The parlor was hung with Currier & Ives prints, and furnished with cumbersome pieces that hugged a Persian carpet. There was a sterile cleanliness about it which can come to a home without children, but the scent of flowers pervaded the air with the sweet malevolence of wreaths upon a grave. Brashear took the settee; Florence sat where her husband had always sat, in a ponderous mohair wing chair which accentuated the image of her as a woman withered and lost.

Judas Cross

Brashear said, "I don't want to bother you, Flo."

"You're not. Somebody from the insurance company is supposed to come by later. I don't care. I don't care about the money, I'm still working."

"Then you're doing all right?"

"I'm going on, if that's what you mean. I hardly see the reason why, but the Good Lord must have wanted it to be this way, and I'm not the one to say He's wrong. Moss will have enough trouble as it is."

"Trouble?"

"For his sins."

There was a glass-topped coffee table in front of Brashear. He leaned forward and nervously rubbed his hand across it, and his fingers came away with dust on them. Dust was something that had never been in this house before. He told her, "I've been thinking about that, what you said at the funeral."

"I shouldn't have said anything, Dan. Please forget it. I was very upset at the time, and I must apologize."

"There's nothing to apologize for. But it's been bothering me, Flo, under the skin. I can't believe Moss was dishonest. He wasn't capable of it. It just wasn't in his character."

"Dan, Moss was like any other man. No reason for him to be different, to be special."

"You can't be sure, can you?"

"No, I can't be sure."

"Why do you think it at all?"

Florence worried an end of the antimacassar draped over the arm of her chair. "A man, there was a man who'd meet him here."

Brashear waited.

"In the afternoons while I'd be at the restaurant. A few times I'd have to come home for this or that, and I'd find them here with the doors closed. But I could hear them, you remember how Moss's voice carried."

"Why was the man here, Flo?"

"I don't recall it word for word. It'd come in snatches, strange and jumbled, but there were things about it, about who gave how much money where, bribes for drugs and gambling and prostitution. Soon as they knew I was around, they would stop and Moss would come out, careful to close the doors so I couldn't see the man. But I did once, once I did."

"What did he look like, Flo?"

"Two weeks ago it was. I walked in on them on purpose. The table there had stacks of money and they were counting it. Moss whipped around like a boy with his hand caught in the cookie jar, and the other man looked cross enough to bite my head off. Moss tried to explain, of course he would, but it did no good. It was so obvious, the glances, the stumbling for lies . . ."

"Flo, this man. Describe him, will you?"

"Odd; he was standing right in front of me, and I can't remember rightly. But I'd say he was short, five-eight or so, and maybe thirty-five, but no more than forty. Dark, very dark. Dark eyes, dark hair, dark complexion."

"What about his weight?"

"I'm not too good at that. He was heavyset, so I'd guess two hundred or thereabouts. He was wearing regular clothes, brown I think, brown trousers and shirt, and a jacket."

"Was it a poplin jacket?"

"It seems so stupid of me. It was a lightweight jacket of some sort, if not a poplin then something similar. It's the effect which sticks to my mind; his meanness, ignorance, his basic cruelty. Dan, he looked like a petty thug, a cheap common crook."

"Well, was there anything *un*common about him?"

"I don't believe I understand."

"Did he have any marks, any scars, anything that would make it easier to identify him? *Think,* Flo."

"Dan, what is this? You're treating me like I was a suspect."

"No, like a witness."

"What are you planning to do, go after this man?"

"Yes."

"You think . . . he might have had something to do with Moss' death?"

"I want to find out."

"Find out about his death . . . or about his stealing?"

Her hand wrung the antimacassar, gripping it in a claw of

tendons, but she didn't notice. Her eyes were steady on Brashear, flat and useless. Brashear tried to meet their look, but couldn't see beyond the hard waxy surface. His voice was soft and empty.

"Both," he said.

"Who's behind it? Who wants it done?"

"Only me, I guess. The squad is satisfied the case is solved, and I'm working strictly on my own."

"Don't. I beg you, don't."

"Don't you want to find out?"

"How can I? I won't stop loving him if he's done wrong, but I don't want to know for sure. I want to keep on hoping that I'm the one who's wrong, and he . . . he . . ." She tilted her face away, pressing her cheek against the chair wing. "He's dead, and I wish I were too."

Brashear watched her, and out of nowhere came the question of how Valerie would react in the same situation—if after the dreams were over, the pain would be this unbearable, and death would extend to her as well—a death of slow and draining anguish.

When at last Flo spoke, it was dull with surrender. "He had a scar. A thin white scar across the forehead, the kind that can never tan. That's all. I don't even know his name."

"Did he ever say anything to you?"

"Not a word."

"Have you seen him anyplace else, like in a store somewhere?"

"No. If I ever did, I'd know him."

"Thanks, Flo."

"But I guess I never knew my husband," she said wearily.

Brashear failed to answer her. He searched for words, for phrases of assurance and consolation, but his mind was empty. There was little more he could do but leave. He stood and looked at her, still not saying anything, and she kept staring down at the rug. The house was thick with fragrance; a heady, silent fragrance that groped to envelop him in a vacuous embrace. She didn't even look up at him as he went out.

Brashear was still thinking about what he could have said to her when he got into his car. If she didn't know Moss, then neither did he . . .

When Florence heard the car drive away, she leaned back with her eyes closed for a few contemplative moments. Then she felt along the rug under the chair, to find the portable battery-operated cassette recorder she'd hidden there when Brashear arrived. Her fingers shook as she switched it on, but then she was calm again. Moss began to speak where he'd left off, continuing a letter he'd been dictating the day he died. The letter was for some mutual friends in Colorado who sent them cassette letters in return, and it was unimportant in content, the family news of the last month. Flo was to have mailed it the next day, but now she never would. She could envision him as he'd been that afternoon, holding the microphone and talking with a large grin on his face, poking fun at everything, especially himself; she would share those last few days together over and over and over whenever she wanted.

"Moss," she whispered to the depthless room. "Moss . . ."

3-b

Brashear kept the tan-colored city bus on a "loose tail," staying a considerable distance behind it. The bus was often as not out of sight, but he knew its route and was more concerned that he alone was following it. Lines of strain and harassment pulled at the corners of his cheeks, and he drove irritably, impatient not to waste any more time than he had already.

Victor Sanchez had been a waste of time. It had taken too long to find the stoolie and puss around with him, and for all of that, Snatch hadn't known a thing. And it had cost Brashear a six-pack of beer to find it out. The dash clock read nine-oh-five, but then it always did, and Brashear figured it was closer to ten-thirty. Valerie would be worried or mad or both, but it couldn't be helped. He'd try to make it up to her tomorrow, but tonight there were things that had to be done—at least, this one

Judas Cross

last thing before going home. The urgency in his chest was a summons he could not ignore.

The bus paused at Thorne and Delaware, a T-shaped intersection with a blind side where nobody could be hidden. A man stood on the sidewalk after the bus pulled away; an obese, almost womanish man who, despite his height, failed to look prepossessing because of his flabby face and bulk. Brashear drove past him without seeming to notice, turned right two blocks later and circled back.

Brashear drove down Thorne again, slowing to study the surrounding apartment complex. A wasteful wind moaned eerily among the units, flattening the shrubs against their vestibules and swaying the old-fashioned street lamps that were strung here and there. Even in the faint light, the moon spending itself fighting layers of dismal cloud, Brashear could see that the man was standing exactly as before, to one side of the bus stop. The wind was moving, the man was not. Brashear cruised up out of the night then, and the man slowly walked to the car and climbed in.

"It's a witch's tit out there," said Racehorse Browne, shivering. "This had better be good."

"That depends on you, Racehorse." Brashear picked up speed, looking about with eyes tensely agitated. "Any trouble?"

"There's never any trouble as long as we meet this way. Only I was in bed when you called. Seems whenever you call me, I'm just sacking out, I don't know how you time it so good. What d'you want?"

"A man, about five-eight, dark hair and complexion, husky. Not like you, but beefy."

"Thanks a lot."

"He's got a scar across his forehead."

Racehorse considered that. "A scar, huh?"

"A thin white scar. Goes with the rest of him."

"I knew a guy like that in Boston once, but his scalp had been peeled way back, leaving it pink. He was the charge man at the Old Howard burlesque house, which is long since gone. He used to come out and spiel the goodies for the candy butchers, singing 'A Pretty Girl Is Like a Melody.' I got to know him pretty good because I was playing trombone for the pit band at the Globe Burlesque. That was on lower Washington Street, if you know Boston. We'd let a skunk out of a box to clear the house between shows."

"Fine. Now, how about the guy I want?"

"Lots of guys floating around like you want. I can't pin down one in particular."

"Well, try."

Racehorse Browne thrust wide his massive thighs, and with a wet sigh, settled against the seat and looked as if he was dozing off. There was a sogginess to him: damp eyes, saliva at the corners of his mouth, a shine to his skin. The street lamps swung overhead in the wind, their light catching the reflection of his watery face in the windshield.

Brashear watched it brighten and fade block after block, and finally said irascibly, "I hadn't planned on the deluxe tour, Racehorse."

"Don't be in such a hurry. Everybody's in a hurry these days, it's bad for you. I was thinking of one, but . . ."

"But what?"

He licked his chops. "How bad're you looking?"

"Thirty worth."

"Thirty, huh?"

"One-time special. What's his name?"

". . . Liz."

"Liz?"

"That's all I've heard him called by. Some guys sure have funny names, don't they?"

"Where's he live?"

"You got me there. All I've done is see him around."

"Where around?"

"Just . . . around. You know how it is."

"No, I don't know how it is."

"Take it my way or not at all."

Brashear pulled the car over to the curb and stopped. "Your way's not worth carfare, Racehorse. What's the matter with you?"

Judas Cross

Racehorse Browne unraveled a filthy handkerchief from his pocket and wiped it across his glistening lips. "Don't get in a knot. I've never done this before, ratting on a guy in the trade."

"He's running book?"

"Yeah, a little, and numbers too, if I get his drift."

"Well, what's the difference to you? You're out of it."

"I've been out of it three times before, and ended up going back for the ride. I'm not making myself no promises I can't keep. That's why I don't like doing this, it's like turning myself in. Only this guy, this guy's too much to take."

"Meaning?"

"Well, it was a couple of weeks back, in the TopHat diner. He was in there with Roache, and seeing's I know Roache, I was invited over."

"Blue Mouse?"

"That's the Roache. So after a while he had to get back, and this Liz stuck around and bought me a cup of coffee. One thing led to something else, and he said he knew I was in the trade and I said I was no more, and then he said too bad, because if I could help him out with a cushion, we could do all right together."

"What kind of cushion?"

"Well, money for one thing, and . . . a little protection. He said he wasn't planning to buck what's around already, but branch out, and that's what sounded wrong-o to me. He wanted to run with kids. You know, teen-agers in high school. Way I figure it, it's a man's own business if he wants to play a little, but kids, they don't know their ass from their elbow. It rubbed me the wrong way."

"Anything else?"

"Not offhand."

"Where's this Liz from?"

"I think New York, but I'm not sure."

"Has he ever fallen?"

"We never spent the time discussing it, but the way he talks and the crowd I've seen him with, it figures."

"Anybody in particular?"

"No, too rich for me. Odds are they could draw you the tier

plan at Ossining." He had the handkerchief scuttling across his face by this time, and his eyes were wide and drenched. "Look, let me off at the next stop going back, will you?"

"Thirty bucks, Racehorse."

"I've earned it. I don't know that much about him, and I'm not about to go asking. Step on toes like his, and you'll get the whole foot in your face."

Brashear stopped the car by the next bus station, and Racehorse lifted himself out with elephantine grace. He turned to collect his money and said in a low, doleful voice, "You wouldn't have gotten this much, only for the kids. It's lucky for you that I've got scruples."

Brashear parked down from the Blue Mouse Theater and walked back toward it, head bent to the gusts. The theater's neon sign was tall and thin, with a herringbone pattern flashing up the sides to where a mouse head blinked, logically enough, in blue. The mouse had too narrow a jaw and looked vaguely corrupt and leering, somewhat like The Joker in the *Batman* comics, but with whiskers. The marquee had permanent fluorescent letters spelling: ADULT SHOW 2–FEATURES–2 NEW SHO EVERY WED. In the display cases at the edges of the foyer were poster cards advertising the features that week: "Tin Lezzie, A Study in Auto-Eroticism" and "A Well-Maid Bed."

He paused and glanced along the street. Five blocks farther on was the Alley Cat, and the thought of the bar brought back that final night with Turnbeau. It was a choleric thought, yellow bile and bitterness which sunk long needles into him; desperately he threw it off. He couldn't continue thinking this way, it would only consume him, paralyze his mind and leave room for nothing else. He turned to the ticket window and the jaundiced woman behind it.

"Roache in?"

She said mechanically, "Three dollars."

Brashear produced his badge. She looked at it with a disinterested eye. "We'll go broke at this rate. Enjoy yourself, freebie."

"Lady, is Roache here or isn't he?"

"In the projection booth."

The booth was unctuous with noise, smoke, lubricant and Roache. He was a ferret of a man, with boot-black Valentino hair and agile hands and feet, and could have been handsomer if his face hadn't been so creased with sharp, hard lines around his eyes and between his nose and upper lip. He was moderately dressed, very pressed of suit and glossy of shoe.

"Hello, Roache."

"Wait a minute."

Roache was at a splicing machine, preparing a strip of film. The booth had cream-colored walls and half a linoleum floor, with two matte-black projectors—one running and the other with its reel housings open—taking up the percentage of space. Brashear peered through one of the portholes. On the screen a naked woman was having ecstasy with a rubber duckie in a bathtub. Roache began winding the take-up reel and said, "Nothing but one break after another. I think this print was done on Saran Wrap."

Brashear looked at him and scratched his beard. "Where's Liz?"

"No cherries around here by that name, sorry."

"It's a man."

"I don't know any drag queens, either."

"Roache," he said mildly, "don't shit me."

"Shut the door when you leave, will you?"

Brashear gazed out the porthole again. The woman had the water frothing now, and the duckie was nowhere to be seen. He said evenly, "I think I'll close you up tonight."

"What?"

"My decency's been offended by all that beaver out there."

Roache smiled a sickly smile. "You're putting me on."

"Why're you fronting for him?"

"I'm not."

"Uh-huh. You want your coat?"

The sound track filtered through the porthole, rank and stale as the smell of smoke and sweat which came with it. Roache stared at the running projector, lids shading eyes that fidgeted. "Liz is nothing to me," he said at last.

"Where is he?"

"Not here, if that's what you're thinking. You can check, you won't find him here."

"What's his real name?"

"Ligarto . . . Yeah, Thad Ligarto, on account it's some kind of family name, bastardized from the Spanish *lagarto,* meaning 'lizard.' So it's Liz for short."

"Where's he live?"

"He's got a pad around here someplace, but I don't know where. The most of it is, he comes in two, three times a week."

"What's the attraction?"

"Nothing. The movie, that's what we're here for."

"He's heavier than that."

"Liz? You're crazy. He's an angler, that's all."

"What's he after?"

"Any corner pocket he can make. Every once in a while he sinks one, and then in a couple of days the wad's gone and he's back on the whine. But nothing big, he wouldn't know what to do with anything big. Not Liz."

"Roache, what's the attraction here?"

"If you told me what this was about, maybe we could work something out."

Brashear didn't say anything. He regarded Roache with a sour, acrid look and combed his fingers through his beard, and the projector chattered and the movie made noises like wrestlers in mud.

Roache started to twitch and finally said in disgust, "Joey. The day cashier, Joey Froelich."

"Serious?"

"I dunno if she's shacking, but she's been out with him enough."

"Where is she now?"

"She gets off at six, so I suppose she's home. I didn't see Liz waiting to pick her up the way he sometimes does."

"What's her address?"

"She moves around a lot."

"The last one will do."

Judas Cross

"No other way?"

"Her address, Roache."

"Glenhaven Trailer Court, number Thirty-four. Christ, now I bet I won't see her again."

"Don't tell me you're part of her action, too."

"Hell, no. It's just that it's hard to find a steady girl to work around here, and I've already had troubles with her. She's been acting up, I don't know why, and threatening to quit. You start throwing your weight around and she will for sure."

"Gee, things are tough."

"I should feel proud, maybe? Big bull like you, you don't hassle the small stuff."

"I have tonight, Roache."

The Glenhaven Trailer Court was not far from the downtown area, on the western lip of the city line. It was flanked by a vacant lot and a service-station parking area, a faded collection of motley trailers that was void of charm or embellishment, and easy to overlook despite the barrenness on either side. Brashear drove through the entrance, which was guarded by two giant Ali Baba jars, and around the circular gravel drive until he came to number 34. The trailer was old and made of aluminum, with rounded corners like a riveted bug. Bricks had been put around the undercarriage to hide the wheels and make a flower bed. The flowers still waited to be planted.

Brashear rang the buzzer beside the door. There was a scrape of a chair, and a sallow-faced man with enormous red ears and a droopy *bandido*-style mustache appeared. He was wearing a once-white pair of coveralls and dark-stained work boots, and there was an oil-company insignia stitched on his breast pocket. He held on to the door handle and didn't look happy about the visit.

"Yeah?"

"I'm looking for Joey Froelich."

"The hell you say," the man said and slammed the door.

On Brashear's foot. Brashear wedged his shoe in farther and pushed against the door, forcing it open. The man lost his balance and stumbled backward, recovered and faced Brashear with his hands poised ready in half-clenched fists. "What's the trick? Liz put you up to this?"

Brashear showed his identification.

The man's eyes hooded and blinked rapidly as if he'd suddenly stepped into a pool of harsh light. "I . . . didn't know. I mean, the way you're dressed and everything. I'm sorry, I didn't know."

"Sure. What's your name?"

"Ralph Dehner."

"You live here?"

"Yeah, I own it."

"And Joey?"

"She . . . moved out two days ago."

"You know where she is?"

"No. You can try the Blue Mouse, she's got a job there. What is it? Is she in trouble?"

"It'd be best if I talk to her."

"I bet it's got something to do with Liz, doesn't it?"

"You know him?"

"Yeah, I do. She threw me over for him."

"Where does he live?"

"I've tried to find out, but none of my friends know—or'll tell me. Joey won't say anything. I've been down to see her—down where she works—but all she'll give me is that she and Liz are in love and for me to stop bothering her. I've tried, but it isn't easy. I really dug her, would've done anything for her. How can you figure it?"

"I couldn't say."

"I never dreamed it would end this way, my girl running around on me, then packing up and leaving. I just about went crazy that first night without her. Had a few drinks, try and figure what to do. I didn't know about Liz then, you see, but I sure did later when I ran into them. I was down where she works, looking for her, went into a diner, the one by the river."

"The TopHat?"

"They were having dinner together there. I was mad enough to've killed them both." Dehner rubbed his chin speculatively.

Judas Cross

The mustache moved as he did, exposing an ugly purple bruise on his jaw. "Ended up tangling with Liz out back, which was a stupid thing to do. I must've been damn fool drunk to try it, but I guess I was lucky."

"How's that?"

"He didn't have to hit me. He carried a gun."

The TopHat resembled a thousand other neighborhood diners: a metal-sided imitation of an abandoned railroad car. It overlooked the Sanponset just below the falls; overlooked the gray, gritty water and eddies of soapy garbage; overlooked it, that is, if you cared to stand on the toilet seat in the can and squint out the tiny window. Truckers went there for early breakfasts, and mechanics and warehousemen for local lunches, and transients for quick dinners on their way to the concrete zoo of alley cats and blue mice. Everybody went there sooner or later. Brashear went there after leaving Dehner to stew in his maudlin juices, because twice it had been mentioned that Ligarto went there. The chance of meeting Ligarto was as tenuous as TopHat's customers, but you never can tell about coincidence.

So Brashear went there and found it had closed for the night.

The lights were out when he arrived back home. Valerie was on her side of the bed, asleep or feigning it, and Brashear undressed quietly in the dark with the guilt of a midnight drunk. He sat on the edge of the mattress for a moment, tense and disturbed, but there was nothing more he could do until the morrow. He submitted to the inevitable and crawled under the cool stiff sheets.

Sleep jibed him. He lay in wait for it, and could hear the purr of gears inside the clock radio abnormally loud, as if they were gnashing within his mind. He tried to strip the facts and calmly scrutinize what he'd learned, but was persistently dogged by the murky relationship between Moss and Ligarto. The two were bound inextricably together.

Ligarto was dregs, but dregs of what remained distorted. The Lizard. Able, evidently, to corrupt the uncorruptible, but ignorant enough to consider Racehorse Browne as a partner in gambling. He packed a gun, but was laughable as anything other than an inept angler by Roache, who should know. Brashear fleetingly wondered what Joey Froelich saw in him. All he could see so far was a tricornered enigma, a conflict of descriptions as though of three different men—but who all wore a poplin-type jacket and might easily have known where to find Moss that fatal night.

Whatever Ligarto was, he was worth tracking. Brashear was committed to run him to ground. He hadn't lied to Florence Turnbeau; there was more at stake than the murder alone. Brashear, resurrecting the scene Flo had described when she'd walked in on her husband and Ligarto, could sympathize with her fears and mistrust. Hadn't Moss kept the secret from himself as well? His own brood of suspicion was busily hatching, and this above all he could not tolerate. He sensed inchoately that he must confirm his basic belief in his partner's honesty and moral conviction—if abandoned now, he would be left empty and meaningless.

3-c

Valerie said, "Don't go."

"Well, I am."

"But you were out to all hours last night, Dan."

"I was home by midnight." Brashear was sitting on the bed, bending over and tying his shoes.

"But it's not even two yet."

"I know."

"You never leave for work this early. Please stay home with me awhile."

Brashear had wanted to leave by noon, but once asleep, force of habit had kept him from awakening until his usual hour. Now he felt agitated, this new turbulence chafing more acutely than ever. He kept his head lowered, able to hear his wife standing beside the dresser—her soft, quick breaths, her flut-

Judas Cross

tering gestures of fingers across wood, her nervous hitch of shoulders as she drew her sweater closer. His own hands were fumbling and clumsy with the tiny pieces of string.

"Something special came up," he said vaguely. "I'm sorry about last night and about now, but it can't be helped."

"It *can*."

"Val, it's my job."

"It's got nothing to do with it."

"I was still half asleep when I got up. Don't go by what I was saying then."

"Don't lie to me! It's something else, something to do with Moss, something you're doing that's against orders. Isn't it?"

Brashear straightened and flexed his foot up and down as though intently considering a new pair of shoes.

"Look at me, Dan!"

He did then, and saw her edgy and distraught.

Very quietly he said, "Yes."

"Oh Lord, what for?"

"I don't know. I honest to God don't really know." He turned away again and looked at the window. The curtains were drawn. He could hear the distant sound of a power mower, a neighbor foolishly grinding up his lawn when the grass was wet. The mower chunked as if snarled, then ceased. It was peaceful suddenly, and hollow.

"Dan," his wife said. She said his name distantly and after some moments. "Dan, don't do this. Think what you're risking, what it will mean to all of us if you're fired. Stop and think."

"I can't."

"You must."

"It's like . . . a molting, Val. Like a snake shedding its skin. There's a new one forming underneath whether wanted or not, and the snake writhes around with its guts being torn apart and it doesn't know why, any more than I know why. Only that it's happening, and the old skin has to be cast off to keep on living."

"You're not making the slightest bit of sense, Dan."

"Sometimes," Brashear said slowly, "sometimes it can't break out and it dies inside."

"I think you've lost your mind," his wife said with shock.
"You're probably right."

Roache was in the box office of the Blue Mouse and was sulking about it. "Up yours, pal," he said to Brashear.
"I never got to Joey last night. Where is she?"
"How should I know? She hasn't shown up today, and now I've got to run it here and the projectors both."
"That's a pity."
"Move on, will you? You're blocking the line."
There was no one behind Brashear.

The TopHat was loafing between lunch and afternoon break when Brashear entered. The booths and stools were mostly vacant, the small windows were steamed opaque, and everything else had a veneer of grease. Brashear sat at the counter and waited for Willard, the ancient day cook, who was at the griddle in front of him.

Willard scooped two fried eggs with the edge of his spatula, his expression that of personal animosity toward them. He hawked consumptively while sliding them on a plate, swallowed whatever it was he'd dredged up while serving them, and then walked the planks back to Brashear.

"Liz been in, Willie?"
"Couple of nights ago, for dinner."
"He say when he'd be back?"
"He comes and goes." Willard knew who Brashear was, if not by name then by instinct, but that was okay by him. He had very little excitement left in his life. He scratched his few stray hairs and let the words sidle out of his mouth. "Between you and me, I just as soon he'd stay away. Real loud-mouth, alla time with the big deal cooking, so he says."
"What's he saying, Willie?"
"Is that why you're looking? Because of this deal of his?"
Brashear shrugged noncommittally. "What do you know about it?"
"Me? Don't look at me, alla know is that he was planning it, whatever it was. I thought he was just shooting his mouth off. If

Judas Cross

I'd thought he was serious, I'd have called the cops myself. I don't want to get mixed up in anything, not me."

"Yeah. Who was he talking to about this deal?"

"Can't say for sure. Never seen the man in before."

"Well, what did he look like?"

"This man? Jeez, I don't remember. See a guy once, that ain't enough, and like I say, I wasn't paying that much mind. Only reason I know Liz is because he's a steady."

"Is Joey Froelich a steady too, Willie?"

"Oh, I see her around. They met in here, you know. Her and Liz, but I never thought they'd hit it off. Joey likes her men strong and handsome. Not that Liz ain't strong, mind you, but he ain't tall either, and he's got a face like hamburger."

"With a scar?"

"A second smile."

"When did you see Joey last?"

"Funny you should ask. It was today, along about noon. She was really carrying a load when she came in, had a cup of coffee to try and sober up, I guess. Not that it did much good."

"You know where she lives?"

"Not regular. But she shouldn't be hard to find."

"How's that?"

"She's staying in the hotel across the street."

The Selwyn was one of those meager hotels that somehow manage to cling like lichen to the cracks between brownstones; the kind which is inevitably up the street from a diner or arcade, and two blocks down and to your left from the bus depot. A small neon sign buzzed to itself above the entrance, the H and O of HOTEL flickering fitfully. The desk clerk was the background figure from an age-yellowed photograph, blurred beyond recognition no matter how long he was studied. Brashear spoke to him briefly, afraid he might crumble if pressed too long, and took the open-caged elevator to the fifth floor.

A young woman answered his knock on room 515. She was tall, about five-seven, with a full-breasted, full-hipped body and long muscled legs like a dancer's. The color of her hair was improbable; Brashear guessed she was a two-tone blonde. Her face was that of a girl twenty-one; but it was showing signs of wear, and at the moment it was the color of early rhubarb.

"Joey Froelich?"

"What's it to you, mister?"

"You know Thad Ligarto?"

"Are you kidding?"

"Do you?"

"Sure I do." She raised the neck of a gin bottle, her grip wavering but determined.

"Put it down, Joey. Is Liz here now?"

"Flake off, creep." She tilted the bottle to her lips.

Brashear impatiently glanced over her shoulder, and then started to brush past her and into the room.

"Why don'cha come in, why don'cha?" she snarled, and swung the bottle at his head.

It came in a lazy swirling loop, and Brashear grabbed her arm, keeping it high. Their tussle was short and wet as the gin gurgled down her wrinkled beige dress in a cascade. He revolved her into an arm lock, Joey yelling, "Help! Police!" and Brashear saying, "I am the police!" He applied pressure to her arm and she strained back against him, groaning, "You're not, you're not. Police! Help!" Then her fingers abruptly slackened and the bottle fell to the carpet. She shuddered and became quite still, as if the loss of the bottle was the loss of her strength, and her eyes squeezed shut and the muscles of her throat worked spasmodically.

"Leggo, leggo, I know when I've had it. You don' have to shove me around, I know when I've had it."

He walked her to the bed, where she slumped in glaze-eyed resentment, and left her to shut the door. The room reeked of gin and mothballs. The furniture was original Grand Rapids, and the window was propped ajar with the spine of a Gideon Bible. The side of the double bed on which Joey Froelich was sitting was rumpled and unmade; the other half sagged under the weight of a large imitation-leather suitcase. Brashear opened the wardrobe, the one other place in the room large enough to hold a man, but the only thing in it was another suitcase that was

Judas Cross

almost the size of a steamer trunk. The bathroom was empty except for an insect trapped in the washbowl.

"Think you're hot, don'cha?" Her voice was a cool, almost sleepy burr. "Think you're hot, beating up a woman."

"Joey, tell me where Liz is."

"He's another one thinks he's hot beating up a woman."

"You?"

"Yesterday."

"Where?"

"His place." She made a vague gesture toward the suitcase behind her. "Said I was in his way, said he couldn't do business with me living there with him. Got nasty about it, called me all sorts of names, said I wasn't a lady. His shins are going to hurt awhile for that one." A fat maudlin tear wormed a trail through the rouge on her cheek. "One crummy fight and he throws me out. Now even Ralphy won't take me back, I betcha."

"Then you won't mind telling me where he lives, will you?"

"Oh, no. I'm not hauling no ashes for him, but I'm not going to blow your whistle either."

Brashear picked up the bottle. There was still a little gin left in it, and he shook it invitingly. "What business is he in, Joey?"

"We never talked about business."

"You fought over it."

She eyed the bottle with the intensity of a predator, her nostrils dilating with thirst. Her mouth moved, and then her voice caught up with it. "Used cars. He was in used cars, every time taking me out in something different."

"Do you own a car, Joey?"

"No."

He handed her the bottle, saying, "You don't really believe he was selling used cars, do you?"

Joey didn't say a word. She cradled the gin between her breasts with a dreary passion.

"You could be facing an accessory rap, Joey."

That still failed to jolt the girl. Her face became tighter, her eyes narrowing into small pinpoints, the bottle hugged more securely to her heart.

"Either here or at the station, Joey."

"If you were more than talk, I'd be there already."

"I'm giving you a chance, Joey. If you're smart, you'll tell me, but suit yourself."

She suited herself by remaining silent. She stayed tight-lipped and mute the rest of the time Brashear was with her.

Brashear stood on the sidewalk outside the Selwyn in morose contemplation. One more facet had been added to Ligarto's image—that of being a booster. Brashear no more believed he was in any legitimate used-car racket than Joey did. Damn that Froelich girl! It was almost as if she'd been reading his thoughts, seeing his essential impotence to arrest her or cause her much more trouble than a civilian could. And now what? A one-man stakeout would be futile; she had no place to go, Ligarto having tossed her out and Dehner being a menace to her. The farthest she'd lead Brashear would be to a nearby liquor store. He had half a mind to tip Dehner anonymously where she was and then see what happened when they got together. But it'd be just his luck that they'd patch things up and stay in bed for a week. No, he'd have to leave her alone in that flyspecked room with her total life packed in two hefty suitcases.

Suitcases.

Bulky, heavy suitcases he doubted she could ever carry by herself . . . Associations continued to link together. If Joey was all alone now, she must have been when she checked in yesterday. No man to help her now, none to have helped her then . . . none to have carried those suitcases for her . . . and she said she didn't own a car. So when Ligarto had heaved her fanny out, how had she moved to the hotel?

A taxi?

3-d

"Don't go," Carberry said.

"I am, Ed."

Judas Cross

"You do, you get out of this car, and you know what it'll mean?"

Brashear sat in the cruiser, his face as putty-colored as the wall of the precinct parking lot in front of him, his heart sullen and resentful and determined.

"It'll mean," he said, "I'll be AWOL tonight."

"It'll mean you'll get yourself busted."

"Not for skipping one shift, Ed. Tell the looie I'm sick."

"Not me. I'm not having any part of this."

"Tell him I've got some rare Korean venereal disease," Brashear said, hoping to joke Carberry into compliance. "Tell him my cock turned green and is falling off."

"He's sharpening the ax to cut it off for you, after what you've done already."

"What I've *done?*"

"You think you could keep it a secret? You think the doc wouldn't bitch? Yeah, and Mrs. Turnbeau wouldn't call after what you did to her? Wasn't Moss bad enough, did you have to work her over too?"

"Did she . . . say why I went to see her?"

"Accusing Moss of having been a thief, something crazy like that. She was hysterical, crying—oh god*damn* you!"

Brashear's face fell awkwardly into a dark, stunned cast. Florence had deliberately sicced the lieutenant on him. He couldn't really blame her, he supposed, hounded as she was by her own vacillating nightmare. For him to continue his brazen disobedience in the face of it, though, would certainly end in his dismissal.

And what had he to show for it so far? No evidence, only the vague supposition that a girl might have taken a cab because her luggage was heavy. He had the hotel as her destination, nothing more. Every other time, he'd had the pickup point and could trace the destination easily through the cabdriver's trip card. But this time, this was a supposition as back-assed cockeyed as the situation itself.

There were two taxi companies in Portlawn: the Checker and the Flying Eagle. The Checker was the larger, so he'd gone there first. After sifting through the logs, he conceded that no

Checker had deposited a passenger at or near the Selwyn the day before. He'd been rooting in the Flying Eagle records when it became time to report for duty. He'd been reluctant to leave, impatient to finish his checking and know for certain, feeling his deduction might slip through his fingers. He'd told the dispatcher that he'd be back shortly, and he'd meant it. Carberry had been pacing the muster room when he arrived at the station, and together they'd walked to the car. Whatever else about Carberry, he wanted to help his partner, to protect him. In that respect, Brashear was grateful. The squad room would have been a lion's den to enter. A martyr he had no desire to be . . .

"I'm warning you, Dan." Carberry's countenance was livid and gnarled. "I kept you away from the looie to pound some sense into you before it's too late. If you don't do a straight night's work like a good boy, you're going to be busted."

The old, cold logic began to seep through Brashear's mind again. He sensed the fearful reasoning which had previously held him checked, wrestling with the vital intuition which had impelled him to this brink. His wife's forebodings repeated themselves, returning to puncture further holes in his quixotic armor. He perceived the cry to play it smart, there's always *mañana*. But behind it all he could feel his decision welling— could feel it opaquely as only an inscrutable force can be felt. He could feel the ethereal rage for action overcoming the calm of deliberation, his hand reaching of its own volition for the door handle.

"Busted right off the force," Carberry said loudly, "not just the squad. You want that, Dan? You want that?"

"It can't be helped. Something's come up."

"You—in front of a review board!"

Brashear got out of the cruiser the way a very old man would, and started walking down the parking lot. His footsteps echoed lonely off the wall.

"You're crazy!" Carberry yelled against his back. "You know that, don't you? You've lost your mind!"

Brashear didn't bother responding to the charge this time.

The garage smelled of gasoline, oil and urine. The cabs looked mangled, the drivers looked mangled, and the automatic

Judas Cross

coffee vendor looked like a battered jukebox. Through the windows of the dispatcher's office, Brashear could see the coffee machine sometimes dribbling something dark from its spout. Behind him was the dispatcher, droning calls over the radio, and beside him was an FBI poster for a suspect, wanted for killing a cabbie. Somebody had pasted the mayor's picture over it. Brashear stood with his hands clasped behind him, smelling the urine and watching the coffee and waiting.

A cab like all the others drove up the entrance ramp. It was a Ford Custom of a dull vermilion, the back door painted with the company name and number, the front with an unfurled black eagle that looked about ready to crow.

"That's the baby," the dispatcher said.

Brashear walked out to meet the cab. "You're Knopf?"

The driver nodded and cracked his chewing gum. Only part of his face was visible through the open window, but what there was of it was oval, coarse-skinned and unhealthily pale. "Can you make it quick? It's kinda slow, and I have to keep rolling if I'm going to make more than my wife tonight."

"It's about a fare you carried yesterday, one you dropped off at the TopHat diner about four-fifteen."

"Don't make no bells ring."

"It's down on your card."

"Well, I guess I did then."

"Was it a girl?"

"Buddy, a person gets in my cab is either male or female, and it goes like that there all day long. I can't remember."

"The next fare went out to Montclair. That's a long haul for you. You'd remember that one, wouldn't you?"

Knopf stared at the headliner and chewed his cud awhile. "Oh," he finally said, "her. Fat broad with a mangy cat, going to a special vet, she said. Must've been special, the way she was giggling and red in the face back there, and one of them— Oh, *now* it comes to me, there was a girl before her."

"About twenty-three, rat-blond, with a couple of suitcases?"

"A real bimbo, that one. Crying and wailing, and the jake wasn't having any part of it, either. I don't blame him."

"This man, what did he look like?"

"A man. He had a head, two arms, two legs. Finish."

"Did he ride with her?"

"It would've been down if he had. He only paid her fare. Threw her in the back and told her to get stuffed, leave him alone, that kind of thing. Then he slipped me a fiver and said to take her anywhere she wanted except around the block. So I did."

"Where was this?"

"Buddy, I was cruising at the time, and he waved me down. It's kind of hard to . . ." He drifted off into the gum chewing, his eyes as blank as cue balls. "It was a small fare, so it was close in. Made a nice tip off the deal, maybe I will again."

"Don't count on it."

"Yep, yep, it was a rooming house, it's coming back that it was a small rooming house. Not far before you get to Laurentide and swing left at the light."

"Can you find it again?"

"You're asking a lot."

"So do you when you renew your license."

"You've got a point, buddy, you've got a point."

The sky was a wet tent, and puddles which had collected on its roof occasionally dripped through the rents. Brashear waited in the shelter of a church entrance until the cab had gone, wishing he'd brought a raincoat with him. The church was a local Roman Catholic branch, its stucco barricaded and its windows meshed as if it were anticipating an atheistic siege. Across Secombe Avenue was a line of houses built when Portlawn was still haughty in the silk-goods industry, set high on embankments to signify distance and position, with porticos and turrets and real shutters that could be folded over the windows. Now the houses had been subdivided into dusty nooks and drafty crannies, converted into a dozen dingy cubicles for a dozen threadbare tenants.

Brashear was studying one in particular, the one Knopf had pointed out. Its once polished wood had discolored to a consistent yellowish gray, like the parchment skin of an agèd man, and

Judas Cross

like an agèd man, it seemed to merely exist now, awaiting a death which had begun to look attractive. He crossed the street and went up the brick steps to the stained-glass front door. There was a row of mailboxes, but none had names, and the door, when tried, was unlocked. The vestibule had an open staircase with a thick wooden banister on the left, an old wall-hung pay phone on the right, and a thick, magnificently scrolled mahogany door straight ahead. In the middle of the door was thumbtacked a sign made from shirtboard and poster paint. It read: KNOCK FOR MANAGER.

Brashear started up the stairs as quietly as he could.

A voice snapped behind him: "I didn't hear no knocking."

Brashear glanced down at an old woman wearing a bathrobe. She was belligerent-eyed and snaggle-toothed, a wrinkled face crisscrossed with centuried grooves. "What're you trying?" she asked crossly. "Sneak a free pad for the night?"

"Take it easy. I'm looking for Ligarto."

"That's what *you* say."

"I'm not staying any longer than I have to, lady."

"He a friend of yours?"

"Ask him."

"I got better things to do than tramp up and down for his bum friends. If you're not out by twelve, I'm charging you five bucks, in advance."

"What's his room?"

"Eight, next to the bath. And don't make no noise, y'hear?"

She was a door slammer.

The banister was shaky, the wallpaper hung in flaps, and the numeral 8 was screwed to the door like a ceramic navel. Brashear kept to one side, reaching across the frame to knock.

"Liz?"

Silence stirred, a mote of soundless dust.

"Hey, Ligarto. Open up, will you?"

Brashear's free hand brushed the holster clipped to his belt as he knocked again, harder. But he felt it to be an unnecessary gesture. The silence seeping from within was too absolute, the dead echo of absence. He quickly glanced both ways along the hall, gripped by a spontaneous sense of exposure, of vulnerability. The bitch had implied that Ligarto was in. Well, where was he?

Brashear stepped away fast and efficiently, like Chandler's wise cat going through a swing door. The bathroom with its noxious odor of ripe disinfectant was empty. The fire-escape window at the end of the hall was locked and sealed with paint. The third and last floor was as below, murmurous with television and conversation, a silence nonetheless. Brashear returned to number 8, hesitated but still heard nothing. He took a credit card from his wallet. Pulling the doorknob toward the hinges, he slid the card in and caught the curve of the spring lock, then jiggled until the lock snicked back and he could push the door open.

"Liz . . . ?"

Light from the hallway peered over his shoulder. It glistened off a bureau mirror and traced the veins of a drawn window shade, outlining the dark icebergs of musty furniture.

Brashear went in as if Ligarto were there.

He made the window, hitting the door shut behind him with his elbow, and swept the drapes closed. He groped his way back to the door, the room a box of ink, and switched on the wall fixtures—thick, fake pairs of candles in gilt brackets, spreading a pale and lifeless glow as if part of a waxwork display. He crouched beside the bureau, sucked in his breath . . . then stood, holstering his revolver. Ligarto wasn't running, wasn't hiding, wasn't in. The landlady was full of crap.

The room was a lament to cheap varnish and tired springs, a melancholy of nighttime promises and early-morning retchings, an incongruity of dead-end lodgings for a man who was supposedly up in the big leagues. Racehorse Browne seemed full of crap, too. A pair of pants squirreled across the bed, a carpet slipper burrowed sole-up beneath the overstuffed chair, bread crumbs infested the lining under the cushion. A small wash basin was bolted to the wall next to the closet, a cake of Ivory dried to the glass shelf above it, alongside a toothbrush, toothpaste, razor and oily comb. On the marble-topped bureau rested a week-old racing form and a glass with the crimson stains of wine. Brashear went through the bureau carefully, a part of him curious over Joey Froelich's masochism, her lust to need a man who'd live in a place like this. One top drawer held a few pieces of shoddy jewelry and some ugly ties; the other drawer had underwear in it. The middle drawer had work shirts and a couple of sweaters, and the bottom drawer was full of dirty socks. Nothing but dirty socks, a ton of them. The closet had the perennial suitcase, a few hangers of sports jackets, slacks and one basketweave suit, and way in the back on the upper shelf, a white flower box.

The box was the kind florists use when sending long-stem roses to your girl. But it was awfully heavy to be holding flowers. Inside the box was the usual layer of waxed tissue, and when Brashear drew the tissue aside, he saw a shotgun.

Jesuschristalmighty.

Brashear found his hands were quivering slightly as he used the tissue to remove the shotgun. He turned it slowly, with the reverent inspection worthy of a prized antique. It was a hammerless, five-shot Magnum repeater, side ejecting with ventilated rib and black walnut grip. It was a neatly sawn Marlin 12-gauge, that's what it was, and damned if somebody hadn't filed off the serial number, but that didn't do anybody any good any more, because underneath would be a second impression of the number, invisible to the naked eye and known as the tattoo. The lab could raise the tattoo by grinding the metal, then etching with an acid-and-alcohol solution. Not that Brashear cared about that right then, not with the shotgun in his hands, and he took it with him and snapped off the lights and found the upholstered chair in the dark and sat down and waited. He placed the shotgun against the armrest and put his .38 in his lap and eased back against the broken construction and rotted stuffing to face the door and wait. He waited the way he should have waited the night at the motel, just sitting possum and waiting.

Waiting for Moss's killer to come through that door.

3-e

Too many hours of sitting in the quiet . . . then the sound of a key scraping the lock, a sound disturbingly acute. Brashear stiffened, raised his pistol.

The door swung wide and hit the side of the bureau. The hinges squeaked sadly as the door slowed to a rest, a quadrangle of light spearing dimly across the dusky floor. A voice came from where Brashear had stood to knock: it was an intense whisper.

"Brashear!"

Brashear thought about moving behind the chair to make less of a target, then thought to hell with it.

"I bumped into Joey tonight, she told me." The voice grew deeper and brassy, yet breathless and oddly lacking the bravado Brashear would have associated with it. He sensed the other's fear instead—the fear and recoil and anathema.

He said almost gently, "Come on in, Liz."

"I knew it had to be you, Moss' partner, nobody else. Did you . . . ?"

"Yeah, I found it."

"I was afraid of that. Soon's I heard you were prowling, I was afraid of that. Stupid of me to've left it here today, but I didn't have anyplace else. You know how cars are broken into these days. Listen, I didn't have to come back, you know."

"Wouldn't have done you any good to run, Liz."

"Not once you turned it in."

"I haven't. Yet." He sighted the Colt where he expected the first movement. "You and me, we're the only ones who know for now. You want to try for it?"

"Suck eggs."

"Come in, Liz. I've got a message for you from Moss."

"Maybe I'd better just highball instead."

"You'll never make the stairs, and that's a promise."

"This doesn't have to be trouble."

"Come on *in*."

Ligarto moved to the frame of the doorway. He was

Judas Cross

lizard-like in eyes only, which were restless and heavy-lidded. Otherwise he was thick-bodied and ox-boned, hefty around the buckle where his stomach bulged underwear through the gaps of a pin-stripe shirt. His dark-brown hair was long and swept back in a mid-fifties ducktail, and other than the noticeable scar, his face was flat and good-naturedly dissipated. Like a pugnacious dog hiding a snarl behind a deceptive grin. He was grinning now, a sheepish grin, while extending his hands in that innocent, palms-free attitude of a magician about to produce a dozen lighted cigarettes.

"I'm not armed, Brashear."

"Turn on the lights and shut the door."

Ligarto moved with a slight stoop to the shoulders, as if being taller than he was and having to accommodate himself to doors and low ceilings. Lights on and door shut, he faced Brashear again, fingers bluntly squeezing the sides of an unzipped green windbreaker.

"Hear me out, you got to do that much."

"Nuts," Brashear said, and rose out of the chair.

"I can explain . . ."

"Don't bother."

"The shotgun. See, I found the shotgun and—"

"Tell me why, no more." Brashear was close now, bringing up his gun. He saw the corrosion in Ligarto's eyes and liked that. "Tell me why you did it to Moss."

"I had nothing to do with him getting it."

"You wanted a bigger share of the action, was that it?"

Ligarto's smile trickled away in buds of perspiration.

"Or did Moss finally wise up and want to call it off?"

"Sweet Jesus, I didn't. We were working together."

"I can guess how," Brashear said viciously. "Oh, I can guess."

"Listen! We were working for Wilcox!"

Brashear blinked heavily, then slipped the muzzle of the .38 into the soft underbelly of Ligarto's throat. "Try again."

"We were! For Joe Wilcox and his committee!"

"But . . ." Brashear shook his head and thrust the gun harder, breaking the scab of a fresh razor nick. Uncongealed blood began to well along the gunsight. "You had me going there for a minute, Liz, I admit you had me going. But I'm catching on fast."

"Listen, for three months we've been working on tie-ins and—"

"You're a chameleon. Fat with numbers and big with the mobs and full of cars and easy women; you're a chameleon that changes shapes instead of colors, and the joke is that you're really none of them. *You're* the joke, Ligarto. A sick, dirty joke."

"Okay, okay, I'm a lot of things to a lot of crumbs. Can't you see, Brashear? I'm whatever it takes to work my way in, gain confidences, find connections. Moss didn't have to, he had it all right there in front of him, and—"

"Stop it!"

Ligarto rolled his eyes, feeling his sweat mingle with the blood and sting his cut skin. "You're not giving me a chance!"

"More than you gave Moss."

"It doesn't matter what I tell you, does it?"

"Tell me the truth."

"I am! Moss and I, we've—"

"Shut up with that."

"It doesn't matter, you're going to—"

"No. Tell me."

But Ligarto was as much an unbeliever as Brashear. He could feel the warmth of his throat pulsing against cold steel, and he lashed out in panic. It was the sudden and convulsive hysteria of a man more front than depth, and it caught Brashear unawares with a wild right and a lunge of a knee to the groin.

Brashear side-stepped, the punch grazing along his molars and slicing the inside of his cheek. He blocked the kick with his thigh and hit Ligarto with a left jab. It sunk deeply into flabby gut, and Ligarto gagged and curled, limply wanting to fold. But Brashear was not finished. Against somebody like Dehner, Ligarto might be king, but Brashear had found his enemy—a flesh-and-blood entity he could see and hear and feel. He hit him in the stomach again, backed him to the door and hit him again. "You lie," he said without much sense, "you turd, you lizard—you lie!" And the hatred, the frustration, the contempt and the resentment, it all surged out of him in short, brutal punches, a roaring in his skull and a seepage of blood in his mouth, each impact delivering a portion of his accumulated misery. Until at last there was none left, and he was able to look at Ligarto clearly again, merely a sagging face with eyes of shock and agony.

Depleted, Brashear let Ligarto sprawl panting, belly down. He gazed at him but the pleasure was gone, the spurt of exhilaration distilling into rancor against himself for having lost control. He holstered his gun and squatted beside the man, knowing he'd hurt Ligarto more in spirit than in flesh, and thankful for that at least as he turned him over to search him. There was a match folder and a pack of cigarettes, a ring of keys, a pair of loaded dice, ninety cents in change and a red plastic comb. The wrist watch was a Timex and the ring was a pot-metal snake entwined around a milk-glass gem. The wallet had a New York driver's license with an address in the city, a YMCA card, a condom, and less than forty dollars in bills. It proved nothing. It was just garbage.

"Liz, Moss would have told me."

Ligarto lay with his eyes closed and didn't answer. Brashear gripped his shirt and yanked him upright, saying, "He would have told me, he would have."

Ligarto's head lolled, seeking the back of his neck, a slurring of noises coming from his lips that sounded like "He knew what you were up to. How could he?"

Brashear released him, his hands shaking involuntarily.

"Moss knew you were on the tab." Ligarto winced sitting up, hesitating there in a sickle curve to allow his muscles to adjust.

"No, you're just saying that. No."

"Don't kid yourself," Ligarto said, and put his hands out to sort of hunch his way up to a standing position. "Only Moss couldn't let on to you that he did, not without telling everything to Wilcox as well." He stumbled over to run cold water in the basin. "That's the kind of guy he was, you can see that much, can't you?"

And that was the crunch.

Because Brashear could see. He saw with eyes twisted blindly inward, toward certain guilty memories festering in his mind. Those goading hints and sermons—Moss must have known. Yet to protect a heel of a partner, he'd avoided the overt accusation, fearing it would force him to lower his own self-imposed blindfold and condemn outright. For Brashear's sake, Moss had purposely compromised himself. The holy man had deliberately grown the clay feet of human compassion, and all the while the sinner had childishly danced with his obvious secrets and transparent ploys.

"I don't know why Moss bothered," Ligarto said, his voice muffled in a towel. "You're one sad case."

Salt rubbed in Brashear's open wound. He glared at Ligarto, his voice thick and stolid. "It means nothing. You still killed him."

"Get off that track, will you?"

"Prove different. Prove *any* of it, Liz."

"I can't prove anything. I'm contracted out of the Reich Agency, and you know those boys. They'd deny their own grandmother if she was working undercover. An agent is dead once he's flushed."

"Too bad. I'm taking you in."

Ligarto spun, throwing his towel into a corner, grayness to his battered face. "I can't, but Wilcox can."

Brashear laughed derisively.

"He can prove where I was that night, and he will."

"You're in clover then, aren't you?"

"It's the last thing I want. Personally, I'd take the rap over sitting with your crew when this hits the fan. But Wilcox will alibi me, even though it'll blow his whole investigation; that's the kind of guy *he* is." The grayness was fading into a pallor now, the cheekbones stiffening. "I don't have to prove nothing. Wilcox will do it for me and get me killed in the process."

"Scared?"

"Damned if I'm not."

"You're stalling, Liz."

"I haven't been telling you about me and Moss to exercise my gums, Brashear, but to save my ass. Listen, you don't know how scared I was coming back here, scared you were setting me up, knowing the way you were loaded for bear."

"I still am."

"Uh-huh. But I'm hoping that whatever Moss thought was in you has got ears. We've supplied plenty to Wilcox, but he's been holding back—wheat from the chaff, he calls it—but you force him to blow the investigation now, and everybody's in for it, good and bad. You take me downtown, and you'll end up with every man-jack with a tin badge on permanent latrine duty. And what about Moss? He was covering for you. Don't you owe him something?"

Brashear moved over and contemplated the shotgun. He admired the way the metal reflected with mellowness, and the graceful curve of the wood. He picked it up. It felt smooth, precise, intense. "I wish you'd try something," Brashear said with quiet fervency. "Something fancy, so I'd have an excuse."

"Not me. I'm Goody Two-shoes. Call Wilcox; do that much."

Brashear placed the gun in the flower box, arranged the tissue and closed the lid. He cradled the box under his left arm and looked at the chair awhile, at the floor, at the blankness beyond. He said softly, "You've got his number, Liz?"

"Yeah."

"It's for Moss."

"I didn't think it was for me. I've got ten cents, too."

Brashear walked Ligarto ahead of him, out the door and down to the pay phone in the vestibule. He made him sit on the bottom step of the stairs, leaning forward with his fingers laced in prayer between his legs, an impossible position from which to attempt anything. He used the number and the dime Ligarto provided, and when a woman's voice answered, he asked for Wilcox, hoping like hell she'd say "Who?" and that it would be a wrong number so he could bust Ligarto good, because it was one thing to be taken for a sucker and another to have to admit the truth of all of this. But she said "Just a moment please" and put the phone down, leaving him with nothing to hear but the keening of his mind.

The landlady opened the door and poked her head out. "What's this? What's this? No calls allowed at this hour."

"Hush up, lady," Brashear said.

"I never!" she sucked in, and slammed the door. A man's voice came on the line: "Joseph Wilcox here"—and Brashear knew he *was* there, recognizing the distinctive voice from past broadcast interviews. It was a voice rich in embellishment and emollient, a voice that came through the wire in 24-point Augustan typeface.

"This is Detective Brashear, Mr. Wilcox."

"What can I do for you?"

"Do you know anybody living in a rooming house on Secombe?"

"Is this Daniel Brashear, of the Falls Precinct?"

"That's right."

"Are you calling from there?"

"From the Secombe Avenue address."

"Mr. Ligarto thinks the pay phone there is hazardous to trust."

"It is. So's his flower box."

There was a shuffling sound, as if Wilcox were rearranging himself. "He was worried a bit ago that you'd find it. I told him he had no choice but to go and find out. Is he in . . . good spirits?"

"Very healthy at the moment. Why was he hiding it?"

"Not hiding, safeguarding the . . . flowers."

"He's been telling quite a story to go along with it."

"To you alone?"

"So far."

"He said he might have to confide in you."

"Is it true?"

"I well imagine."

"All of it?"

"I'll clear him of any charges arising from your partner's death, if that's what you're referring to."

"And what about my partner, Mr. Wilcox. What about Moss?"

Soft breathing crept from the receiver.

"Was he a Judas, Mr. Wilcox?"

"A what? Is that some of your departmental slang?"

"Judas." It was a ball of barbed wire in his throat.

"Was he? A Judas betrays innocents for money, I believe. Detective Turnbeau came to us out of personal conviction, and it is absurd to term the men he reported as innocents. Isn't the police department more of a Judas when it sells out the innocents it has sworn to protect?"

"You're twisting words."

"I'm asking you to define your labels."

"You're asking me to ignore what's going on."

"Am I?"

"I won't be another Judas for you."

"Perish the thought. In the age of reason, it's heresy to hold faith. But you'd better consider the situation pragmatically."

"Your man has filled in the blanks," Brashear said tightly.

"Then all I can do is reiterate the obvious."

Brashear leaned against the phone box and looked stiffly at Ligarto. Ligarto hadn't moved a muscle other than around his mouth, which had that ugly mutt grin on it again. Brashear waited for it to go away. It faded slowly. Then he said, "I'm keeping the box."

"No, you're not. You're going to give it back to Ligarto."

"Why do you want it?"

"We're going to run some tests, determine what we can."

"That's what police labs are for."

"And your findings would be more complete, I'm sure. But I doubt they'd help Mr. Adam any, if they indicated his innocence. That's why we have plans to use other, less official channels."

"And if Billie Dee is linked, what then? A vanishing act?"

"Hardly. Miss Rainey has already made it clear to you that we don't know whether to plead him guilty or not. This will help. Our information will immediately be made public. The whole point of this is to make sure it *is* made public."

"You know what you're doing is against the law, don't you?"

"There's no evidence yet showing the . . . was used in a crime. And if the box itself is concealment of a weapon, that's a far cry from the injustice possible if it were under police wraps."

"I'm keeping the box," Brashear said again.

"Don't make a mistake. Give it to Ligarto."

"Not now, not ever."

"You're forcing things you don't want and can't handle."

"I don't care," Brashear said coldly. "Flat out, I don't care what you do. I care that I've got a lead to Moss' killer, and I'm going to take it downtown where it belongs and put it through the wringer. All the way through."

"*All* the way?"

"And what's left in the wash gets hung on the line." Brashear tongued the cut in his cheek and added, "If you don't believe me, that's too damn bad."

Wilcox asked slowly, "What happens to Ligarto?"

Brashear didn't answer for a time. He studied Ligarto some more, and Ligarto blinked with his canine expression of eager suffering, eyes shiny as rabbit pellets under water. It all boiled down to one fact for Brashear: Moss was his pivot and had to be redeemed. This was blood, Brashear knew, not reason; deaf instinct overcoming deafening logic. Yet rather than being disruptive, the realization was strangely calming to him, as when after a fever, the awareness of being sick is proof of recovery.

He said, "Keep the leash on him. If I want Liz, he'd better be available."

"No, it's no good." The voice on the phone became soothing, the way fur is stroked. "I understand how you feel, but give the box back and step aside. This has to be played out the way it was dealt."

"I'm in the game, Mr. Wilcox."

"You're too late. You weren't around when it was dealt."

"Let's say I'm sitting in for a missing friend."

A shutter banged somewhere outside; inside, the air was foul. Wilcox spoke very deliberately, very evenly. "Take the trick, then. But don't take it any differently than you say you are."

It took a couple of tries to jab the receiver back on the wishbone, and the flower box rattled slightly when Brashear picked it up. He walked to the front door and opened it, turned to where Ligarto still sat, smiled a wooden smile and said, "Let's step out on the porch where it's private."

Ligarto unfolded and followed heavily. The neighboring windows winked with light: rain and wind slashed them in the face. In the dimness of the porch, Ligarto's face was fat and sassy with half-closed eyes. "Sudden change of plans, eh?"

Brashear said, "As a cop, I hate it. I've got a feeling I'm going to hate it more later on, but for now I'm taking a chance on you. The box is coming with me."

"You don't hear me complaining. It's been a pain."

"Let's hear how you got it."

Ligarto dusted his right pants leg. "Well, this nosing I've been doing, it got me out to Anchor Auto Wreckers."

"The big one on Route Forty-six?"

"Uh-huh. I was out there the night Moss got hit, only I didn't know it at the time, of course. This dark-blue Merc pulls in like it's on fire, and the next thing I know it's in line for the crusher. I thought that was funny, seeing as it's only a year old, so when I got a chance I took a look, and there was this shotgun on the back-seat floor. There was nothing I could do about the Merc, but I was able to sneak the shotgun out and hide it in some scrap metal."

"What did the driver look like?"

"Can't say. He drove it in the yard and then was gone, wham. Nobody I recognized, anyway. Only reason I took the gun was—well, you know how it is, something smelled funny. So then there was the problem of how to get it out of the yard, and it was Wilcox who came up with the flower-box idea. I went to the yard bragging about this new girl who dripped like a tenement faucet at the sight of roses, and the first couple of times they checked me, the flowers were there. Then they stopped checking me, and the fifth day I went with the box empty."

"What was the license number of the car?"

"Oh, that won't do you any good."

"Why not?"

"Listen, that's why I'm there. What they're doing at Anchor

is crushing junkers but switching the bills of sale and license transfers to new cars of the same make and model. It's like swipe-to-order, some of it done by—well . . ."

"Say it."

"Some of . . . your boys pick up a new one every once in a while when they're out cruising. I've been down there the last few weeks scratching loose change when they've needed an extra hand, trying to get a permanent berth, so I know about the branding they do. You know, engine and factory numbers filed off or leaded in, and the numbers from the junkers used instead—and the Merc was one that had already gone through the yard once before. So I know the number, sure, but it's phony. The rub for me is that I haven't been able to trace where the cars go after they're repainted and shipped out. I drive them sometimes, but no place special, not that the dames mind a change of iron. I guess that's what Joey was yapping to you about, wasn't it?"

"I guess it was."

"Good kid, got too serious, though. I had to move her out anyway so I could bring the box in to hide for Wilcox, but she was always talking about getting married, and there was nothing between us. Just something to kill time. I wouldn't marry her on a bet, you can believe that."

"Coming from you," Brashear said, "I can. Now, what was the license number of this Merc . . ."

3-f

JVSTITIA HONORIS PRAEMIVM

It hung etched in the crust of the building, but Brashear was all the way into the muster room before he realized he'd passed beneath it. Without flinching. Without so much as an upward glance at the precarious motto, and it had been an age since he could recall having done that. A goddamn coon's age.

" 'Lo, Andy."

Fratelli didn't answer. There was no "Yo," not even an

automatic one, coming from behind the high-propped book hiding his face. There was only the protest of his chair and the turning of a page. A taint of a smile curved the sides of Brashear's mouth, and went away. He walked toward the stairs, passing a group of patrolmen coming from the lockers, the men mostly newer recruits before his time, familiar by face if not by name. Their faces edged away from acknowledging his, oddly alien. Perhaps they hadn't noticed him, as Fratelli hadn't noticed him . . .

He climbed the steps to the Detective Division, snapping his thumbnail against the end of the flower box under his arm, the taste of irony metallic in his mouth, and a turmoil, damp and obscure, in his chest. Noise came through the squad-room door, of typing, of chatter, of the ringing telephone—but when Brashear walked in, the noise stopped as if gutted. Carberry wasn't there, but Schmidt and Nalisco, the new man Pantages, and Robard; they all turned to look at him, and then they all looked at one another and flared up again amongst themselves. None voiced interest in Brashear or his box. He stood by the railing and was alone, totally alone, in that noisy room.

Lieutenant Jules's door was slightly ajar, a harsh white light leaking from around the other side. Brashear glanced at his watch and noted how late it was for Jules to be in, and the almost wistful smile returned as he thought of what he could expect from him. Scraps of phrases leaped with anticipation: insubordination, failure to carry out orders, willfully ignoring regulation this of section that . . . the lieutenant wouldn't be interested in what was in the box, either. Brashear glanced around, unconsciously taking stock of the familiar, settling his mind to the reality that he would soon be leaving it forever. The box under his arm wouldn't change things that much; he'd stirred up too much resentment, bruised too many feelings. The eyes were not smiling as before, but were cold and distant. The voices of men once friendly were now despairing and repellent.

He walked in without knocking.

Lieutenant Jules raised his head. His gray suit seemed without a wrinkle, his shirt crisp and the tie perfectly knotted, the hat perched on his head as if especially fitted for Brashear's entrance. Only his face appeared worn, and that as stone would be, the color bleak and indifferent. He spoke with the cords of his throat. "I've been waiting to see if you'd show."

"Yes, sir." Brashear sat down and balanced the flower box across his knees.

"Weren't you assigned with Carberry?"

"Yes, sir."

"Weren't you told to lay off this other thing?"

"Yes, sir."

"Weren't you—" Lieutenant Jules stopped, took off his hat and clutched a half-gallon container of milk from atop the refrigerator. He drank directly from the spout, ignoring the glass empty on his desk. He asked in a grim and low voice, "Do I have to make a list?"

"It's not necessary."

"How much damage you've done is anybody's guess, the way you've been screwing around. You haven't broken too many laws yet, so we can keep this strictly a departmental matter. I guess we can be thankful for that, right?"

Brashear muttered, "And then there's the law that's man's own."

Lieutenant Jules cupped his ear. "I didn't catch that."

"Forget it."

He scowled, setting the milk carton down hard. "What the hell has gotten into you, Brashear?"

"Nothing."

"Nothing! I'm ashamed I ever laid eyes on you," he fumed. "You're a disgrace to everything holy, and what's been the point of it? Nothing? Nothing at all?"

Brashear splayed his fingers across the lid of the box, unable to voice a defense. He'd never been able to with the lieutenant, but this time it was not out of fear. Fear has an element of hope and indecision to it, and he was fully aware that nothing could be done for him, and that his future was irrevocable. Nor was it a concern for Moss and Ligarto, nor a smugness for having the shotgun to spring. What held him mute was what he did *not* know, what he found incapable of putting into words. He couldn't explain the force of dark blood which

Judas Cross

had been the spur to his actions. It was uncharted, the jungle of instinct surrounding his tiny settlement of conscious mind; and they were unidentifiable, the untamed beasts who roamed its vast interior. Suffice it to say that they were there, they were him, all of him, with an integrity to the whole which could not be denied or dishonored.

Lieutenant Jules, still scowling, mistook the stillness for ignominy. "Nothing you can say, is there? Whatever you figured you were doing, it can't be softened or explained away. I'd hoped you'd take my hint before, but I can see I was wasting my breath."

Brashear remained quiet, as fire can be when in walls.

The phone rang. Not loudly or insistently, but every fifth second it would ring. The lieutenant let it. Presently it ceased, and he leaned his elbows on the desk, his eyes protruding like peas from a pod. "You're suspended, pending review. Give me your badge."

Brashear unpinned the metal shield from his wallet. "Ther're some dents in it," he said, sliding it across, "but less than most."

"By God, but you need a trimming!"

Brashear leaned back in the chair, smiling that thin, sardonic smile again. "There was this idea that the car Arlen Hilton saw might've been stolen. I checked out the hot sheet two days on either side, and came up with a list of cars that fit his description and hadn't been located yet. Then I sent word out that I'd pay fifty dollars for each one found. Sometimes that works. Well, one kid reported a dark-blue year-old Mercury out on Quincy."

"Who's the kid?"

"Doesn't matter now. He was hustling the fifty to get out of town before some bigger boys could lean on him. He's gone. At first I thought it was a bummer, being as the Merc wasn't on the hot sheet even, but I ended up paying him."

The refrigerator started up, rattling the window blinds. Lieutenant Jules said testily, "You're not expecting a refund, I hope."

Brashear's eyes got lean and tight, but he kept his tone mild and conversational. "What interested me was that Quincy is not a street on which to expect a new Mercury. But it was there, and when I went through it I found out the plates were off another car, and that it had been repainted recently."

He took a piece of paper out of his pocket. On it was the license number Ligarto had given him. The lieutenant took it and looked hard at it, chewing his teeth together like a dog without a bone to gnaw.

"And then there was this, in the back." Brashear stood up and laid the flower box lengthwise on the desk. He removed the lid and took out the gun and placed it very gently in front of the box, then closed the lid and put the box under his arm again.

"What'd you bring that thing in for?"

"You might want to check it," Brashear said and headed for the door.

"What? Why?"

"I'm not sure, but it might be the gun that killed Moss."

"What? Wait a minute!" Lieutenant Jules raged behind him. He shut the door swiftly and kept on going.

The stairs were a narrow path leading to the canyon floor of Harrison. Save for the half-whispered tread of an occasional car and the lingering hiss of wind, he was isolated in the dark. He hugged his jacket closer against the antiseptic chill, dispersing the squad and his pain, forgetting the bitter relish of the muster room. When Brashear had passed Fratelli this final time and said good night, Fratelli still refused to answer Yo. He spit.

The car was still warm. Brashear drove to a cocktail lounge and picked up a fifth of Fleischmann's rye, and in a little while he was home. The street was empty and the house was still. He went into the house as he always did, quietly so as not to disturb the sleeping, got a glass from the kitchen and walked into the living room and put the glass and the bottle on the table beside his easy chair. He took the flower box, which had been under his arm the whole time, and set a match to it in the fireplace. He watched it for a moment, and because the crackle and flame seemed comforting to him, he added a couple of Presto-logs to keep the blaze going. Then he sat down and cracked the seal.

He drank the whiskey as the lieutenant drank milk.

Judas Cross

It hadn't been a bad story as stories went. It must've sounded suspicious to Lieutenant Jules, but it was as close to the truth as he could come without involving Ligarto or Moss, and he hadn't been able to think of anything better in the short time he'd had. The shotgun was wiped clean of prints, other than perhaps his own, for Ligarto had manhandled it enough to ruin anything of value. The only other link was burning cheerfully. He'd been canned as he'd been warned he'd be. Brashear refilled his glass, feeling a bit silly for drinking this way, but there was nothing to keep him company save his morbid thoughts.

What could he turn to? All he knew or cared about was police work. To be forced into some menial job because he'd tried to be his father's kind of cop seemed particularly galling. Then there was Valerie, she'd have her say. He hoped it would be in a rampage rather than lament; a bravely suffering woman can be a debilitating thing. He hadn't been much of a man for her these years together, faltering and acquiescing before every whip except his own. It wasn't her fault if she'd lost faith in him, but a woman without faith in her man is a sabotaging crutch, emasculating as she dutifully bears her angelic burden. A curse cloaked as a blessing. Needfully he took another swallow, suffering from one type of hangover and determined to get another.

He heard a rustling sound and glanced from the fire. Valerie had come into the living room unnoticed, and was standing to one side of the portieres, her eyes fixed solemnly on him. She wore her robe loose and her hair flowed unbound. It was as if she'd risen from her sleep and was still in the midst of a dream. A bad dream.

"I thought I heard you come in," she said.
"Yes." He poured a drink.
"Are you coming to bed?"
"In a while."
"You . . . did it, didn't you?"
"Yes," he said, and drank the drink.
"You're not on the squad."
"I'm not on the force."

She made a small, moaning sound and wrung her hands together. "You knew it, you knew it, but you went ahead and did it anyway. Dan, Dan, no job, no money, disgraced in the community—did you want this for your family?"

"The Pariah of Wiletta Lane."

"Don't be flippant! We've worked hard for a nice home and nice things. I don't want to be ruined and lose them all. Why did you do it?"

"Do I have to have a nice, tight reason for everything I do?"

"Yes, when it's as serious as this."

A piece of burned log crumbled in the fireplace, flaring for a second and sending streaks of flame through her hair.

"Did you know," Brashear said after a long while, "that the chief inspector for New York City's Department of Buildings was arrested for soliciting a bribe?"

"Dan, put down that bottle and—"

"A bribe to approve an elevator in a child day-care center?"

"—*please* talk sensibly?"

"This man, in a top position of public trust, would take money not to look carefully at an elevator whose riders were all little children. Or that our honorable U.S. representative from Hudson County recently pleaded guilty to evading nearly seventy-five thousand dollars in taxes? Well, Val, that's my reason, because what they were doing was wrong. It *was* wrong, wasn't it?"

"Deplorable, but—"

"I haven't been any better. Takes a thief to catch a thief, so the best cops are crooked cops. Can't do a better job if I weren't dishonest, laws being the way they are these days. If you haven't heard about the others, Val, you've heard me say that stuff enough."

"We've talked it over a thousand times."

"Little talk, working out the little arguments. I bet the building inspector and the congressman had their fancy arguments all worked out too. Trouble is, it still doesn't make it right."

"What you've just done is?"

"Right. Cap-ital R. Can you hear the capital R, Val?"

"I hear drunken rubbish."

"No such thing as an absolute Right, but there is. There is for me, and do you know why? Ask me why, Val."

Valerie sighed with great magnanimity.

"Because I believe there is."

"That's the silliest thing you've ever said."

"The only answer. Any argument, no matter how logical, can always be reduced to 'I believe' if asked enough 'why's.' Well, I short-circuited the semantic crap and went straight to the source. I believe I've done Right. But don't ask me why, Val, because I can't answer that last one. Nobody can."

"What am I supposed to do now?" Her nails clawed at her robe, her voice rising like a scalpel. "Applaud your genius? You're drunk and disgusting!"

"True, true."

"You don't care what you throw away or who you hurt. For heaven's sake, stop this drinking and come to bed. Tomorrow you can see what you can do to patch things up. Maybe if you go down and apologize and promise to behave they'll take you back."

"Too late. And if it weren't, I wouldn't."

"You have to do something before you destroy everything."

He laughed without mirth, and the rye burned in his throat. "We haven't built, we've been collecting, collecting to keep from building. Material to hide behind, but don't worry: as a fence it's self-destroying."

"I don't even know you when you're like this."

It took some effort, but Brashear got up out of the chair and removed his pants. He thrust them toward his wife. "Here, put them on."

"Whatever for?"

"To see if they fit."

"You know they don't. They're too big."

Brashear sat down abruptly. "They are from now on, Val."

"Dan, I could . . . could *leave* you when you're this way!"

"The ultimate threat." Over the rim of his glass he smoldered out at her. "Could you?"

"Is that what you want? Are you doing this on purpose so I will?"

Perhaps it was the whiskey, but Brashear thought he could detect a demon malicious behind her pining eyes. A pious demon, ready to diminish him should he weaken. He moved his lips, but the liquor was behaving like Novocaine, and he had to speak with soft, careful enunciation. "You can cry now if you want."

She made a slow, strangled sob in her throat. Face niveous, she turned and blindly plunged down the hall to slam the bedroom door.

Brashear settled to the glow of the fire, feeling very warm inside and out.

"Mercy, mercy," he sighed, and poured himself another drink.

3-g

Hands and voices dredging him back.

He started up growling, as an animal suddenly awakened and still lost in its feral mists. But it was only Valerie, only her prim voice insistent and her soft hands shaking. He stared up at her, saying nothing.

"When you're presentable, come into the kitchen." She turned her tight face from his. "Your lieutenant is here to see you."

"What about?"

"I wouldn't know." She bit one of her knuckles and left the room.

Brashear sat for a time, his head dry and flaky as though filled with sand. The clock on the mantel was out of focus, but by the light slanting through the windows he guessed it was somewhere around noon, not that it mattered. He probed weakly with his hands and found his pants, the empty bottle rolling off them as he picked them up from the floor. He put them on and sat down a while longer.

The door to the kitchen was closed when he made the hall. He didn't pause but went directly to the bathroom and washed his face. His reflection glistened in the mirror with eyes of shadowed pink. The Alka-Seltzer tasted like soap and so did the toothpaste. He walked back gradually, massaging his left temple and trying to think of a way to avoid the kitchen, but nothing came to him.

The light in the kitchen was too bright. He squinted until he could slide into the breakfast nook across from Lieutenant Jules and cup his cheeks in his hands. He didn't look at anything, especially not the light. Nobody said a word.

Lieutenant Jules was moody in his gray suit. He fiddled with the brim of his hat, which rested on the table next to a glass of milk, and gazed gravely at Brashear as only a frog can. Valerie was at the stove with her back turned, stoically acting as if she weren't in the room at all. Or if she were, as if she couldn't care less what went on. The only sound was the percolator bubbling, and then she picked it up and poured a cup, brought it over and put it in front of Brashear.

"Anything else?" Her tone was clipped and trim.

"No."

Lieutenant Jules cleared his throat. "A hangover, right?"

"Yeah. Blame me?"

"Not very. I miss them myself now and then." He shifted to gaze out the window at nothing in particular. "It's been drizzling this morning, but it's supposed to clear up later."

"You didn't come here to pass on the weather forecast."

The lieutenant picked up his glass and sipped some milk reflectively, his face still averted. "You did it to me royal, you know. You shoved it in and broke off the handle."

Brashear said coldly, "Talk to a mirror, not to me."

"You're cute. I never did take to you much."

"If it's any consolation, I did it to myself too."

The lieutenant turned back and set the glass down with meticulous care. "The shotgun checks out positive. FI is working on the tattoo, if they don't have the number already. I've been closeted with the commissioner since nine this morning. I had to lay it all out for him, every lousy scrap of it, including the fiasco with your report. He's ordered Adam released, which is the only thing he could do, considering. I guess you're not too sorry to hear that."

"Not so far. What's the rest of it?"

"We traced that license number, and it's to a car that was junked months ago. We're following through with the wrecking yard. The car you saw on Quincy isn't there any longer."

"I didn't think it would be."

"The commissioner questions your story and so do I. I don't like it very much. In fact, I think it stinks."

"I'm not overly fond of it myself."

"You want to change it?"

"Not especially."

"You're making it tough."

"That's a pip. I get canned bringing in the only solid lead anybody's yet found, and you say I'm making it tough."

"You can't be so stupid as to be holding out, but you can't be as dumb about it as you say you are."

Brashear looked at him with blank eyes.

The lieutenant said, "You ought to come clean, but it's no skin off my nose if you don't. I'm out of it."

"You want some more milk?"

"No, I don't want any more milk."

"I want some more coffee. Val?"

Valerie was at the sink, washing the same plate over and over as if its design were a hated stain. A firm-lipped wraith in skirt and sweater, her face white plaster underneath her make-up, she brought the percolator, then faded back to the sink. Brashear glanced from her to the lieutenant.

"This sure went sour awful fast," Lieutenant Jules said thoughtfully. He reached into his suit pocket and took out Brashear's shield. The metal winked in the light when he put it on the table, his stubby fingers turning it around like a jigsaw piece needing to be fit.

He said, "You're back."

"On a platter, I am."

"That's fine with me, but this is for the commissioner."

Brashear watched the badge for a moment, then said, "The

commissioner wants one less club that Wilcox can hit him with, that's all."

"Not a bad idea, but it's the wrong one."

"The hell."

Lieutenant Jules opened his mouth as if to snap at a fly, then closed it again and spoke through his teeth. "Is there anything anybody can tell you?"

"I can't come back. You know that."

"The suspension is dropped, squashed. It never happened."

"The one thing worse than bucking the system is to buck it and be right. I'm a leper."

"You won't be in my squad, don't fret."

"I can't be transferred far enough away to make a difference."

"By God, what do you want—for me to butter it?"

"I want Moss' killer." Brashear spoke calmly, coolly. "I want the real one, not some rapper it can be hung on. The rest of it I'll worry about later, maybe when I'm asleep."

"You can't do it from out there, now can you?"

Brashear tensed. The cup in his hand shook only a little.

Lieutenant Jules frowned, his massive face a corrugation of lines. He returned to fondling his hat. "We're not on the case any longer. The commissioner has turned it over to a couple of hand-picked boys from Metro—and you, if you want to climb down and slum."

"Who are they?"

"Laird and Macklin. Know them?"

"Of them. The Best-Dressed Kid."

"Don't let Macklin hear you. There's more to it than that. The commissioner is raw as an oyster over this Wilcox investigation. If Wilcox has his way, the works will be torn down and nobody'll respect the department. It won't matter if the charges are true or not, or how many of them are, every cop will rate the big razoo, and that's no good, right? So he's set up a special task force to see if we can't pull Wilcox's teeth before the showdown."

"Nice—after consistently ignoring the corruption."

"So it's politics, but give him his due. A general doesn't

always know what's going on as well as a private does, if you see what I mean. Soon as Wilcox started rolling, he got the task force organized on the q.t. It was like pulling *his* teeth to tell me this morning, and I never once guessed it before, he's kept it that secret. He's a fine man, the finest I've known, Brashear. We went through the grades together and I stood at his son's bar mitzvah, and I think that's the only thing that saved me from discharge. He's not buying his way out, he's fighting what is worth defending, for the good of the department and for the good of the city."

"And Laird and Macklin are part of this task force?"

"I don't know who the others are, and frankly, I don't want to."

"And if I . . . ?"

"Permanent assignment."

Brashear had a sudden desire to laugh unpleasantly in his face. "Oh, that's rich! A Judas!"

"We're not begging. Nobody's needed that bad, but if nothing else," the lieutenant said sarcastically, "the commissioner can be sure you won't buckle under the pressure."

"He wants me to be a Judas!"

"Shut up you, shut up." Lieutenant Jules drank the last inch of milk, patted his mouth with the back of his hand, notched the creases in his hat and stuck it back on. His face remained solemn, but his eyes were slate and his voice was the whetting of a scythe.

"I've known in the back of my mind what some of the men have been doing, and I've known it was bad to keep it in the back of my mind. Maybe I've been kidding myself that a good job the rest of the time would make up for it, but it hasn't worked out that way. Too much loyalty is like the tar baby; it can suck you in, hold you down. It sounds dirty to me, cop against cop, but I guess the commissioner is right. If we don't clean our own house, Wilcox will take us all to the cleaners."

Brashear smiled at the ceiling, tugging on the shaggy growth of his beard. He thought of Moss, and what his dead partner would say if he could know about this . . . and then he

Judas Cross

lowered his head, his eyes lidded with wariness. "How does Moss fit in with this task-force thing?"

"He's the carrot. Your carrot."

Brashear lapsed into silence again, thinking about it some more. There wasn't much to think over. For him to be away from the action right then seemed wrong to him. It was for the most practical and yet the most emotional of reasons, because what he believed in was trouble, because the fighting was an internal battle and it would be good to be a part of it. It was no more complicated than that. He leaned over and plucked up the badge. He rubbed it on his sleeve.

"I'm enough of an ass," he said quietly, "to bite."

"I'll tell the commissioner how pleased you are."

It was said snidely; Brashear ignored it. "When do I get together with Laird and Macklin?"

"Search me. I suppose they'll call, once I get back to the commissioner." Lieutenant Jules rose, awkward and uneasy. He patted his pockets and cleared his throat. "Well, I . . . I guess that's it."

Brashear showed him to the door. The lieutenant stood on the porch and shuffled his feet. "I'm out of it," he said again, and Brashear, not knowing what to say, nodded his head.

"I've told you all I know," Jules said. Halfway down the steps he added, "And I'm forgetting that much as of now." He walked ponderously away, his mouth slightly agape.

Brashear closed the door and walked back to the kitchen. He looked at Valerie, and she began to cry. The tears rimmed her eyes and she wiped them away and then she started to laugh.

"I'm so proud of you! So damn proud of you!"

"What?"

"I've been a compromise too, haven't I?" She looked up at him with those extraordinary blue eyes, and slowly her pink tongue tipped up to caress her lip. "I have been, haven't I?"

"But no longer."

"No, no longer." Her voice was a sigh, a breath, a fragrance as she pressed against him. "It was a cold night for me last night."

"When's Lisa get home from school?"

"Not until three . . ."

She leaned back against his encircling arms and he sank his face between her breasts. She murmured, I felt I'd been wronged but my virtue is only as deep as yours, it is yours, and we are as one. I want you, Dan, take me, take me. The once caustic light outlined her long ripe nakedness while he gently stroked her glowing flesh, the color of wheat with buds of red and roots of gold. His resentment toward her, his bitterness and anger against his work washed from his heart, and he lay in her arms of passion until he slept, contented.

3-h

Laird was driving.

Laird, it seemed, always drove. He drove his own middle-aged Buick convertible as if to do battle, too much brake and too much steering, a constant patter of mutterings and asides and snowflakes of cigarette ash, a man who concentrated on his driving and swore he would master it, and who should never have been allowed behind a wheel. It was the only time, of the few times Brashear had been with him, that Laird looked fierce. Normally his features were as bland as his rumpled suit, and ludicrous for a cop—fine auburn hair, soft cheeks, a wide, flat nose, and eyes that were brightly cynical, as if polished by years of merry sinning.

"You drive worse than I hump," said Macklin, who sat in the back, leaning forward to rest his arms on the front seat. He was a tiny man who, when standing, barely came to Brashear's shoulder. He wore a cinnamon-colored wool suit cut long and tight over the hips and full across the chest, with exaggerated lapels. His feet were incredibly small and encased in highly polished wing tips, and his hair lay in perpendicular swaths on an egg-shaped skull. It contrasted sharply with pale, almost translucent skin which was pulled taut and thin over delicate bones. He liked it when you made a mistake about his size. Then he could break your back for you.

Brashear sat in the front at an angle against the door, with his sports jacket unbuttoned and a turtleneck sweater tucked into clean slacks. "It worked out fine, Dan, picking you up at your house," Macklin went on to say to Brashear. "Just as well you didn't come down to Metro."

"No need," Laird said. "We've been cooling our heels most of the day. The Marlin factory didn't phone us back until nearly two-thirty, it took them that long to trace the serial number."

"The shotgun was part of a shipment made a year ago to Isher Gun Shop, here in Portlawn. You know the place?"

Brashear said no, he didn't.

"It's on Isher," Laird said, and flicked his cigarette in the general direction of the ashtray.

Neither he nor Macklin had yet to discuss the task force or Brashear's recruitment. They'd skirted the issue, touching upon it lightly with the wariness of strange dogs sniffing each other. Brashear considered this understandable and didn't push it. It would develop in time, with relaxation and familiarity. This was sufficient for now, with his peace and faith to savor.

The Buick lurched down Straight Street in East Portlawn, moisture on the pavement echoing back the sound of the tires. Behind them was the bridge across the Sanponset; somewhere ahead was the Purple Cow, where Kitt Rainey had fought her childhood. It was picturesque, Straight Street. The hustle of merchants died with the bridge, becoming an endless Sunday of neglect. The cars were few and older and mostly passing through; the stores declined to shops, and shops to doors nailed shut and windows boarded over; and empty lots blossomed into patches of colorful fungus, the used-car dealer. The few pedestrians were in keeping, gliding lean and furtive as African fennecs, or impassively shambling, dulled with eroded eyes.

"It was on our way to your place," Laird continued suddenly. "So we stopped, and damned if the clerk didn't find a sales slip."

"Coughed it out of a file," Macklin added. "That's what they do with gun sales, keep the name and address on file. Couldn't read the name, it was just a scrawl. Wasn't it around here you found the car, Dan?"

After a pause, Brashear said with indifference, "Yeah, over a few blocks and further up."

"Uh-huh," Macklin said, and dropped it.

"Lucky about that sales slip," Laird said.

"The address will be a phony, it always is on them things."

"Yeah, but you got to check it out. You never can tell."

Macklin asked, "You play poker, Dan?"

"What's an inside flush?"

"Well, that's good. We're all beginners here. Hey," he said, tapping Laird on the shoulder, "feel up to a game tonight?"

"Sure, I can always use the change."

"You should live so long. But the wife's going out to some gabfest, so we'll have the house to ourselves. What was that address?"

"Seven thirty-seven."

"You passed it."

"No, I didn't. I've been watching."

"Well, the bakery there says Seven thirty-nine."

"Christ, so it does. Now how could that have happened?" Laird veered the car into a parking spot, ran one wheel up on the sidewalk and stalled the engine. He fumbled with the ignition key, but Macklin told him to forget it, he'd only make it worse.

Sodden puffs of wind followed them as they walked down the street erratic with odors, skimming puddles and dancing litter, dying without a trace to live again a moment later. Next to the bakery outlet for day-old bread was a tire retreader's, and next to the tire retreader's was a hot-dog stand, and next to the hot-dog stand was a Walgreen's drugstore. That was too far, because Walgreen's was 729.

"See?" Macklin said irritably. "Ain't no such animal."

"Let's be sure," Laird said with stubbornness, and stopped at the hot-dog stand. The stand was a counter with a window, a couple of fryers and a griddle in the tiny room behind it. A man sat staring out the window. He didn't move, he didn't read, he didn't do anything except sit and stare out the window, a little

Judas Cross

old man whose face had the color and texture of a prune. Brashear was reminded of a stuffed owl under a bell jar. Laird tapped on the glass and the man raised the bottom half of the window.

"Is this Seven thirty-seven?"

"No."

"What's this here?"

"A dirty hole someplace else," the man said and shut the window.

"Rat bastard," Macklin yelled at him.

The man curled his lip and showed a row of dirty horse teeth. He made a gesture with his thumb, indicating the back of the stand.

"What's behind it?" Macklin asked unnecessarily.

There was a small alley between the stand and the tire retreader's, lined with garbage cans and windows scummed over, and shadows laden with the cloying scent of refuse like the perfume of an old whore. The retreader's ran about a hundred feet farther than the back of the stand, a sagging board fence behind which rose a mound of bald tires. That was on the right; to the left was a rectangular field, tacky and weedy, hemmed in on the other three sides by the blank walls of buildings. In the center was a small square shack of unpainted wood, with a corrugated roof sloping down with an inward slant, looking weatherbeaten and lost as a sleeping wino, and closed tight enough to have lockjaw.

They stood at the end of the alley and looked at it.

"Well?" Laird sounded pleased with himself.

"I dunno." Macklin rubbed his nose.

"Nobody's there, more'n likely," Laird said.

Brashear said quietly, "One way to find out."

"And I'm not in the mood to be polite about it." Macklin slid out his service revolver. "Give me a couple of minutes."

He hunched over and ran swiftly along the fence. When he reached the end of it, he paused rigid and wary for the first hint of detection. Nothing happened. He flashed a smile and sprinted into a stretch of scrub brush that extended behind the cottage.

"We'll give him another minute to get set," Laird said.

Brashear stood in the dimness, alert but hearing nothing. The only movement were the flies and gnats over the garbage cans. It was almost too quiet. It began to bother him, though he couldn't tell why. It was going well so far, smoothly and efficiently and with a few of the breaks going their way for once. Yet something about it didn't satisfy him, something distant and ominous which flicked tenderly at his mind.

Laird said, "Now."

Brashear darted forward, the obscure forebodings reaching out for him. Angrily he dismissed them, listening and watching all the time, his .38 a comfort in his grip. He reached the door, the porch soft with rot, Laird like a blocker close on his left. There was still no sound other than the groan of the porch, and then there was the sharp rap of a gun going off. A single shot inside the shack, thick and meaty as if from a heavy caliber.

"Break it in!" Laird urged breathlessly.

Brashear surged against the edge of the door with his arm and shoulder, then pivoted and kicked the plate below the knob. The door splintered open. He followed it in, crouching, pistol ready. His eyes swept the room, the one room of the cottage—dim and claustral it was, the walls weeping moisture and the ceiling showing lath in spots. The furniture was spindly and meager, and the floor undulated as if twisted by the currents of time. A smell of cordite stung his nostrils. Then he saw Macklin.

Macklin was standing next to a chair, languidly holstering his revolver. In the chair was Billie Dee Adam, sitting casually as if fallen asleep over a dull book. One arm rested in his lap, the other dangled limply. His open eyes were shallow and glassy as they inspected the hole in the middle of his chest. The hole was scorched and rimmed with turbid red, and there were lines of blood staining his shirt a muddy brown.

"This must be his place," Macklin said.

Despair clutched Brashear as he stared at Adam. For a split instant he was held fast, rooted with the climax to a premonition he'd felt since crossing into East Portlawn. Adam had been guilty all along. And he'd set the man free, to potentially kill again. His crusade for justice had been a dangerous farce, and the squad had been right from the beginning, while he . . . He

Judas Cross

had reached the rock bottom of hopelessness, the end of faith itself. The instant lingered, endlessly stretching . . .

Macklin said, "I didn't shoot him, Dan. Laird did earlier, when we were supposedly at the gun shop. We only said that to make it look good."

Brashear jerked his head up, not understanding. Then he saw the sawed-off shotgun propped in one corner, and he did understand. It was *the* shotgun, the one used on Moss. One quick, helpless glance . . .

Macklin raised the .22 pistol he'd been holding in his other hand. "Adios, scumbag," he said gently, and shot Brashear in the face.

An atavistic scream tore from Brashear, driven by the terror of panic and the horror of truth, the entire truth. He stood for a moment dead but alive, watching Laird come around with his gun still drawn, and Macklin press the .22 into the dead Negro's hand, and then he went softly to his knees to fall back on the floor, his mouth open and convulsing blood. It was a setup, a double cross for Judases, and he would die as a hero shooting it out with a killer, and the records and memories would be suitably altered, and the papers would eat it up alive. But Adam had not killed Moss—no, that had been a setup too—and if Ligarto wasn't a corpse by now, he soon would be because it was all over, all over and unraveled. Brashear thought of Lieutenant Jules for a second and wondered if he was in on this, but the vision faded into inconsequence as the commissioner took his place, the commissioner with his private task force to clean up the department, clean it up of troublemakers and Judases.

He lay on the floor but the room became dark like his bedroom in the night and he thought he was home and lying in bed with Val curled next to him, and it occurred to him that maybe it was near dawn and Val would be getting up quietly the way she did so he could sleep, and he wanted to turn over to tell her how much he loved her but he couldn't. And the dreams were all confusing and he felt that he wasn't able to untangle them and tell Valerie he was lying on a stinking floor in a stinking room somewhere and to let him sleep for another few hours please and let him dream. The air was crowded with old faces and blurred figures and heavy voices like the one that said, "Just like Moss."

And then another that resembled Macklin's took its place, blurred and indistinct. "Too bad. He could've made a good cop."

And then the pain went away and so did his dreams.

About the Author

JEFFREY M. WALLMANN was born in Seattle, Washington, two days before Pearl Harbor, and has served the prerequisite apprenticeship of motley jobs all writers must, including a stint as an undercover detective in New York. He has had a number of stories and softcover books published, mostly mysteries, but some western and science fiction. He lives on the Côte d'Azur with, he says, "a cold apartment, a ratty car, and a sour stomach from too much cheap wine." He is currently working on his next novel.